Supernova

Supernova

First published in Indonesian under the same title
by Truedee Books, Bandung, 2001
English edition copyright © 2011 The Lontar Foundation
English language translation copyright © 2011 Harry Aveling

Publication of the Modern Library of Indonesia Series, of which this book is one title,
is made possible by the generous assistance of the Djarum Foundation.
Additional assistance provided by the Ford Foundation

Template design by DesignLab; layout and cover by Cyprianus Jaya Naipun
Cover illustration: *Caught In A Barrier of Sharp Rocks* by Lucia Hartini
Image courtesy of the OHD Museum of Modern & Contemporary Indonesian Art
Printed in Indonesia by PT Subur Printing

ISBN No. 978-979-8083-83-9

MODERN LIBRARY OF INDONESIA

DEWI LESTARI

Supernova
— The Knight, the Princess and the Falling Star —

Translated by Harry Aveling

Jakarta, Indonesia

Thirty-three Fragments of Content

SUPERNOVA

– For those who want to LIVE –

Welcome.

What you are about to read will not always be easy to understand. In *Supernova* we will be talking about billions of years of history. We will follow the movement of something that moves faster than light. We will deal with things that can only be dimly grasped by abstract faith yet nevertheless live deep down in the shriveled-up cells of our minds.

Please be patient. Within every complexity there is always a simple pattern each one of us can understand. Perhaps it is so simple that our intellect, which for some reason always tries to make everything as complicated as possible, will not be able to accept it. Even so, we will try to study it, to understand how one simple act can destroy all complexities.

I am not a teacher. You are not a student. I simply want to show you the facts. To unravel the spider's web. To untie the knots in an endless silver thread.

There is one simple paradigm here: wholeness; moving toward one goal, the creation of a better life, for us, for the world.

Supernova is not an occult text. Not a religious institution. Not a course in philosophy. *Supernova* includes many things—history, myth, science, your supermarket receipts—to show you the nodes in the silver thread of the network of life. Process this information through your own individual filter and adapt it to your own place in reality.

This is a kindergarten, an opportunity to play with life: to live!

In this relative universe so full of uncertainty I can only guarantee you one thing: changing the way you see life will have an enormous impact on the world, one far greater than you could ever imagine.

1

What Is, Is

The two men sat facing each other. There was warmth in their eyes. The feeling was still real. Ten years had done nothing to diminish its essence. The flames may not have burned as wildly as they once had, but the fire was still very much there: a warmth that promised to last forever. And isn't that what we are all looking for?

They had met in Georgetown, right under the street sign at the start of Wisconsin Avenue. Washington D.C. was bathed in the heat of the summer sun; each man had arrived with his own group of friends and their first meeting had been rather ordinary.

"Hi! I'm Dhimas. From George Washington University," he said, introducing himself. His pink complexion made him look like a baby.

Ruben took his hand. The skin was soft. He suspected that Dhimas regularly used skin lotion. Ruben never pampered himself. His face was hard, lined by the sun and by ageing. His grip was strong. "Ruben. From Johns Hopkins Medical School."

"How was the drive down from Baltimore?"

"Really smooth."

"I hear that 295 North beyond New York Avenue is shut down."

"We came by way of George Washington Park."

His tone was almost arrogant. Dhimas could tell that Ruben was a cynical scholarship kid, an introvert whose best friends were his books. Dhimas' completely opposite style told Ruben that Dhimas was an Indonesian who had more money than ways of spending it, the sort of person whom he ordinarily didn't like at all.

But that summer day had a special quality, which made people act out of character. Even though the two groups had never hung out together, they were all shipwrecked in an expensive apartment belonging to one of Dhimas' friends in the Watergate Complex. The evening began with a good meal and continued on to various chemical desserts. Soon guests lay sprawled on the sofas, carpets and even in the bathtub. Waves of New Age music washed over the apartment, covering the voices of the two men as they talked.

"This is my first serotonin storm," Ruben said, gazing into the distance. "God, this is amazing."

"Serotonin storm," Dhimas repeated with a goofy smile. "I like that."

"How can those guys sleep? There has never been a moment like this before. It's a whole new beginning!"

"Are you on something the rest of us don't know about?"

Ruben looked around. How could he explain it? He had finally found the mirror he had been looking for all his life and was enjoying his own reflection. *Don't ask me to say anything just yet.*

The French mathematician Benoit Mandelbrot had opened the door to a new understanding of the meaning of turbulence. The first time Ruben read Mandelbrot's work he gained an insight into the beauty created by the harmonious union of the known and the unknown, of order and chaos.

No matter how perfectly a system is organized, chaos lurks close by, like a tenacious doppelganger. As soon as the system reaches a critical point, chaos is unleashed. Even in a system that seems to be in perfect equilibrium, chaos and order are both present, like whipped cream holding together the layers of a cake. That rich, delicious cream is the quantum zone, an infinite jungle in which everything is relative and is both potential and probable.

In daily life, chaos takes the form of intermittency, discontinuity, fracture. For centuries, reductionists dominated science without ever bothering to study this phenomenon; they saw the world only as black and white. But then, one day, they entered the grey arena of quantum discourse and were shaken to their core. For those who worshiped objectivity, relativity was as terrifying as Judgment Day. Science could no longer be purely objective. Sometimes at least, it also had to be subjective.

What are you, turbulence?

Where are you hiding?

Ruben imagined turbulence to be like the dark border around frames in a reel of film. As soon as the film is running at twenty-five frames a second the border vanishes; the separate pictures cease to exist; the connection between them disappears. In reality, turbulence works like a transcendental kitchen, not bound by time or space, endlessly intersected by a multiplicity of non-local signals, snaring all kinds of probabilities, potencies and quantum leaps. All kinds of definite and specific life soups are served from that kitchen; they make up the reality that we taste and smell. But even when we know that turbulence is everywhere—from the life of a simple bacterium to the myriad interactions of the stars in the Milky Way—it is still difficult to fathom existence as a totality or the whole of existence. It is also difficult to see disorder as anything more than the crackle of a poorly tuned short-wave radio or the static on a television screen after the night's transmission has finished.

Science itself was suddenly subjected to turbulence. Whether scientists wanted to or not, they now had to concede that both order and disorder arose from the one Vast Absence of Order. They had to admit that the brain is a non-linear organ and that the heart beats in an irregular manner, that these irregularities create the order that appears to characterize human existence.

Just like any other system, Ruben's system of thought depended on attractors continually regulating self-directed feedback, a process constantly moving backwards and forwards, creating an amplified system. When a certain point of flux is reached, there is an opportunity for change. The phase of uncertainty reaches its peak and something called bifurcation occurs. At this point, a whole new stage of evolution takes place.

That night a hurricane shook Ruben's solar plexus. He could feel something seething in the sympathetic network around his heart and within his being. He had reached his own point of bifurcation.

A subtle insight settled in his soul and amplified his understanding. What had previously been scattered fragments of an intellectual system suddenly came together. And in the middle of this living room, the universe revealed some of its secrets before his very eyes.

Ruben saw a mist slowly cover everything in the room, reaching into the farthest corners. He watched darkness and light work together to form the reality of the material world, like pixels that form colored patterns on a television screen. Energy fields were everywhere, flowing out from every wall. He couldn't help laughing. *Life is fluid.* Life flows steadily and effortlessly like a warm current in a great ocean and he was part of that stream, being carried along in its center.

Ruben cautiously raised his hands, overwhelmed by the mist. His body was nothing more than a projected image. And when he identified with the pixels and not with his body, Ruben realized that he was immortal. There was no beginning and no end; no cause and no effect. The only thing that exists is existence itself. What is, is: continually moving, expanding, evolving.

Ruben thought he would explode. He wanted to laugh and cry, all at the same time. "I can see everything so clearly. It is so pure. Everything is interrelated but nothing belongs to anything else. I understand it all. There is nowhere to go, everything is already here," he stuttered as he tried to explain what he was seeing.

"Ah, yes," Dhimas observed confidently. "No more questions about time, whether you passed the course, finished the assignment, aced the quiz..."

"Oh, come on!" Ruben replied harshly. "I was talking about the Einstein-Podolsky-Rosen paradox, Lorenz butterfly, electronic duality, the paradox of Schrödinger's cat..."

"The zombie cat? Half dead and half alive?"

"I know how to reconcile materialism and idealism! Materialism and non-materialism; and science and religion. I can see it all," Ruben babbled. "All because of serotonin."

"No kidding."

"Do you know that people who meditate are simply building up serotonin in their brains?"

"So that's what we're doing?" Dhimas asked. "Meditating? Cool. So easy. Just swallow. You don't even have to control your breathing."

"It isn't easy at all. People who meditate produce serotonin naturally. They don't use external help the way we do. There are no short cuts, remember that. You think this doesn't matter but our bodies are building up huge debts that sooner or later will have to be repaid."

"Please, give me a break. Don't turn this into a bad trip. Your mentioning Einstein and a zombie cat was enough of a downer."

But Ruben didn't seem to notice the insult. "Dhimas, I'm starting to think that serotonin is some sort of mental detergent. Do you agree?"

"How would I know? You're the one who is studying at Johns Hopkins."

"On a night like this, you can be anything you want."

"I'd like to be a poet."

"You can be an astronaut, you know."

"If you would glimpse the beauty we revere, look in your heart and its image will appear. Make of your heart a looking-glass and see reflected there the Friend's nobility."

Ruben stared at Dhimas in disbelief. "Have you ever studied chaos theory?"

"Sorry, chaos theory? I was quoting from a poem by Attar, a Sufi mystic."

"Sufism, chaos theory, relativity, quantum physics... Sometimes I think they all came out of the same Pandora's box, except that they emerged at different times and in different places. Can you feel how beautiful the poem is? How it connects with what I just said?"

"What did you just say?"

"That your new truth came after you saw both sides of the mirror. Not just one side. And the mirror is very close to each one of us."

"In our own hearts?"

"I would say in every atom of our bodies."

"That's amazing. Only problem is, you never mentioned any of it."

"What do you mean?" Ruben asked, surprised. "Didn't I just explain Mandelbrot's ideas to you? And tell you all about turbulence?"

Dhimas shook his head and giggled. "You're in worse shape than you thought."

"Wow!" Ruben gasped in amazement. "It wasn't just me talking to myself, was it? It must have been real, it felt so fuckin' real! Serotonin, you're amazing!"

Dhimas cast a quick glance at Ruben, prone on the couch beside him. "I salute you and your understanding, Ruben. Most people think these experiments are only shallow entertainment."

"You guys got too much money, that's all. When you run out, all you have to do is call Mommy and Daddy and everything is fine again. In this regard, the wealthy and the poor are the same: neither can appreciate life fully."

"You're just full of yourself. Because you're on scholarship, I suppose."

"And I'll bet your old man manages a big conglomerate or is a four-star general or a diplomat; that your major is marketing or business administration; and that you fly to Indonesia every summer- and winter-semester break just to bring back boxes and boxes of IndoMie instant noodles to put in your shiny kitchen cupboard."

"I'm taking English lit," Dhimas interrupted. "And I never go home for summer because I always take summer classes or special courses. Don't assume too much, dude. We're not all the same."

Ruben grimaced. "Sorry."

But Dhimas wasn't offended and was already thinking about something else. "Ruben, did you say that serotonin is like some sort of mental detergent?"

"It was only a hypothesis, a metaphor at the very least. Why?"

"You might be right. My head feels really clear. And I want to be honest with you about something." Dhimas swallowed hard. "I'm…"

"Gay?" Ruben cut in.

Dhimas gasped. "How did you…?"

Ruben laughed out loud. "It was obvious: from the friends you hang out with, from the fact that you live near Dupont Circle! Did you really have to get high before you could admit it?" He laughed again.

Dhimas laughed too. He felt foolish.

"Relax. And you thought I wasn't?" Ruben asked casually.

Dhimas gasped again. "But you can't be, you look so…"

"Look so what? So manly? Who says all gay guys have to dress fashionably or speak with a lisp? I just am what I am and I came out more than a year ago. My parents know about it. They accept me. They said that if I have to be roasted in hell with all the other citizens of Sodom and Gomorrah, they'll ask Yahweh if they can join the grill too. If I'm defective, it must be their fault. Aren't they great?"

Dhimas couldn't say a thing. He had met his hero at last.

Ruben's thoughts had stopped spinning. "I want to make a promise. You be my witness, OK?"

"What sort of promise?"

"That in ten year's time, I will create write something that will bridge the gap between the various branches of learning."

"Ten years. That's a long time away."

"Time flies, my friend."

"Fine. Ten years for you and ten for me. A wide-ranging novel that will move a lot of hearts."

"So help us God."

For a long time, neither man said anything. Their minds ran freely toward an undefined future, ten years hence.

"Hey!" Dhimas suddenly exclaimed. "They say that this damned chemical substance can remain in your body fat for years."

"They're right. That means we'll relive this moment one day. Amen to that!"

"I hope that when this moment returns, we'll still be lying on our backs like this… together."

Ruben turned his head too find the most sincere smile he had ever seen curving on the lips of the blushing baby-face he had met only hours ago at the top of Wisconsin Avenue.

Ten years had passed and the smile was still there: the proud smile that had tracked him on the podium when he graduated *cum laude*; the gentle smile that encouraged him to rest for a while after he had pulled an all-nighter writing a seminar paper; the confident smile that had followed his triumphs and difficulties throughout his career as a college professor.

Ruben, the Indonesian Jew whose glowing enthusiasm set other people on fire, was still Dhimas' hero. And he was still a quantum psychologist, a vocation with a job description to unite the theories of psychology and cosmology in a way that only he could understand. Nevertheless, Ruben was the perfect critic for Dhimas, constantly challenging him with fresh ideas and unique perspectives. Every article Dhimas wrote, every lecture he gave benefited from many hours of discussion together.

That night at the Watergate they had experienced their last serotonin storm together. For the next three months and twenty-one days, they endured a different storm: an endorphin storm, the love hormone.

Remarkably, although they had now been an item for a decade, Ruben and Dhimas never wanted to live together, the way other couples did. When people asked them why, they replied that they could but would rather not. They liked the idea that they needed to make an effort to be together.

Ten years had passed in the twinkle of an eye.

"Happy tenth anniversary, Dhimas."
"Happy anniversary to you too, dear soulmate."
A warm city breeze made its way surreptitiously through a window into Ruben's living room. It was a simple house in South Jakarta. The interior design was plain with racks of books stretching from floor to ceiling, all packed tightly with volumes arranged in

alphabetical order. The only reason Ruben didn't call his house a library was that he didn't want to appear pretentious.

There were no flowers on the table, no box of chocolates. Although this was their tenth anniversary, there was only a stack of papers and a heap of ballpoint pens.

"So," Dhimas said as he put on his glasses, "we agreed to write this masterpiece together. And not in the form of an academic article but as a story."

Ruben shot Dhimas a reluctant look.

"Stop that, Ruben. An article would be too hard to chew and, forgive me, would be deadly boring as well. At best, it might make a good handout for one of your classes. We need to write something a lot of people will want to read. A poetic romance with a bit of science thrown in. Right?"

Ruben raised his eyebrows, then he too put on his glasses.

"Good," Dhimas said. "We can package it as an unconventional love story. Make it controversial, full of social and moral conflict."

"Let me guess," Ruben yawned. "A gay love story."

"That could be interesting, but no. The subject of homosexuality is still off the radar for most Indonesians. I want to write about an ordinary heterosexual couple, faced with a really difficult situation. Let's say that one of them is married."

Ruben sighed heavily, "Even worse; a total cliché. But I guess it does give us something to work with: religion and morality. OK, I agree."

"Which one of them will be married: the man or the woman?"

"The woman," Rubin replied firmly. "If the man was married, people would merely think that he was a sleaze or a leech. And Muslim men can have four wives anyway. There wouldn't be any conflict."

"Demographics? Age, sex, location?"

"Under forty. Our main characters must be young, urban, cosmopolitan, technologically sophisticated, with good information-processing skills. There is no point in writing about tramps or some quaint villagers. It is the young professionals who will make or break Indonesia."

"Twenty to thirty... living in Jakarta... educated... professionals." Dhimas carefully wrote down the details.

"Jakarta. Agreed. Opposites creating more opposites. Caught by Eastern politeness and desires, with the West pushing them to behave badly."

Dhimas snorted. "Look who's talking. We're everything you've just said, we even studied in the States, ground zero of modern capitalism."

"Sure, we were among the lucky ones who had the chance to measure ourselves against global culture; to struggle with it and to seek knowledge in other places and cultures. But a lot of people fail dismally. They waste their parents' money. Others get their degrees and become mere robots."

The two men worked steadily throughout the afternoon. Their progress was marked by Ruben's many cups of coffee and ideas which flowered one after the other....

Later as they recapped their conversation, reviewing the issues and the characters of the work, Dhimas remarked: "Earlier, Ruben, you suggested the introduction of an avatar. What in the world does an avatar have to do with our ticky-tacky love story? I mean, an avatar is like God taking human form, isn't it. Hello?"

"Don't forget that in a system as complex as nature, nothing is trivial. Most people are only interested in the grand scale. At a certain point, a love story can reflect the experience of the whole of society. Individuals are always shaped by their society, aren't they?"

"I see. The avatar represents the neutral aspect that can reconcile everything."

"Point zero. Neutrality with attitude," Ruben added.

Dhimas became excited. "Great! Let's work on this avatar."

"Be patient. The avatar comes last. Let's deal with our heterosexual couple first. The man. Let's start with the man."

"He has to be handsome!" Dhimas insisted. "That will make me want to write about him more."

"Obviously he has to be intelligent and successful—successful through his own efforts—and he should work in an environment full of conflict, under pressure the whole time…"

"A multinational corporation. What else?" Dhimas shrugged. "How successful do we want him to be?"

"Successful with a capital 'S'. Cream of the crop. Let's make his job really important. That will increase the pressure."

"Although, deep down he has the soul of a poet."

"Dhimas!" Ruben protested.

"That will make things more interesting. Let's say some minor conflict when he was a child separated him from his natural ability to express himself. He is a robot. Very successful but very empty. One day, he meets the Princess and everything changes. We can use the change that takes place in him as a way of questioning the whole nature of love. He can be like a sophisticated computer, super-organized, which is suddenly infected by a virus. And there's no Norton Anti-Virus either, right? The couple will be trapped, with no way out of their situation. We can just bring everything slowly to the boil, then watch it explode." Dhimas' eyes shone.

Ruben was immediately attracted to the idea. He knew that when a system was overloaded, it reached a point of bifurcation before beginning to move in a new and different direction. The story they were proposing was like the classic tale of Epimenides the Cretan who had said: "All Cretans are liars." The question of whether Epimenides was telling the truth was one that could trap even the greatest computer in an unending logical paradox. There was no way of deciding between yes and no, because both answers were correct.

Ruben disagreed with the functionalists who insisted that people think like computers. The brain is hardware; our ideas are the software. If that was true, no one could think about Epimenides without going mad. The only way to resolve the paradox was to jump outside the system. Make a quantum leap. Something only an intelligent system could do. A machine couldn't.

Ruben smiled contentedly. There was a quantum gateway in Dhimas' description of the main male character. "All right, we can make him a poet. Though I don't really know how to make him both a poet and a senior executive in a multinational corporation."

"Don't worry. That's my business."

"What will we call him?"

"Let's decide that later. Otherwise we'll quarrel for ages. For the moment let's call him 'the Knight'."

"The Knight who fights for the love of the Princess. Who fights against society and has to kill the dragon." Ruben paused, then he added mockingly, "How romantic."

Dhimas smiled. "The Knight and the Princess. A classic love story. Is there a place for couples like us in the land of fairy tales, my love?"

"Of course not. We followers of Socrates belong to history. We don't need fairy tales."

The two men sat facing each other with warmth in their eyes. The flames may not have roared as wildly as they once had, but the coals radiated a heat that promised to last forever. Isn't that what we all want?

2

The Knight

After parking his car in the garage of his house, Ferré remained in the driver's seat, carefully checking his things, one after the other, not wanting to leave anything behind: his briefcase, papers, *The Harvard Business Review*, the charger for his cellphone, his glasses' case.

He continued searching, now for something else. Why hadn't he put it in a safe place, he asked himself. He groped in his shirt pocket, then sighed with relief. Pulling out a small and misshapen pencil stub, he smiled. It was as if he could see her face.

The telephone inside his house rang. He ran to answer it.

"Hello? Oh, Rafael, it's you! Calling on my house phone? You crazy Ambonese bastard. I thought it might have been someone important."

Ferré's close friend, Rafael, chuckled at the other end of the line. "I'm bored. Do you want to go out somewhere tonight?"

"No, but thanks for asking. I've got a lot of work to do. I have a series of meetings with our mutual friend next week."

"Who? That white guy?"

"None other! Your former vice president. How unlucky can my company be to have recruited him as its regional president? And I'm the lucky guy who has to report to him every fucking month."

"Well, it's Friday tomorrow! C'mon, let's go somewhere, chill out a bit, what do you say?"

"What difference does it make if tomorrow's Friday?" Ferré muttered. "In another two days it will be Monday and I will have to deal with him for the entire week. I'm jealous of you. Sometimes I think I should resign and open a repair shop like you or something, anything so that there are no more hierarchies, no more long meetings."

"Bullshit. That's total crap, Ferré. Just admit you enjoy being busy. You are the complete professional, control freak, always planning something. You're as much a multinational blood-sucking leech as that white guy is. I bet that if you were ever where I am now, you'd be breaking your neck to get back to your office. And your long meetings."

"I'm not so sure," Ferré laughed.

"We could go to the gym tomorrow night, talk in the steam room like two boring old farts."

"Why are you so keen to do something?"

"Lala has this family thing out of town in Anyer, so I'm all yours. What do you say? I could think of better things to do, you know. But I'd rather hang out with *you*."

Ferré cut the conversation short. "I'm flattered. But, really, put me last on your list for a while, OK?"

He needed to relax.

Standing under the shower, Ferré watched the silver drops splashing around him. He was daydreaming, something he never used to do. A man like him needed to stay focused on business but tonight his thoughts were elsewhere, as they had been every night for the past month. Rafael would have split his sides laughing if he knew that Ferré was daydreaming.

Rana... Ferré wrote her name on the steamy glass. He was like a teenager in love for the very first time, who wanted to write his sweetheart's name everywhere.

Ferré had lied to Rafael. He didn't touch his work. Rana had taught him, indirectly, to appreciate spare time. Now he was happy to sit around in his tee-shirt and shorts, watch television, drink tea, and play with his dumbbells while he read a magazine. When his body and mind were relaxed, he could daydream longer about Rana.

Ferré looked at his watch. It was almost one o'clock in the morning. Obviously he couldn't ring her, not on her cellphone, not at home. Which was why he needed this kind of moment: to recreate what he couldn't immediately reach out and touch, to allow his imagination to be stimulated by a simulacrum and to satisfy himself that way.

Ferré realized that he was monotonously running on the same spot. No matter how happy he felt he was always equally disappointed and this haunted him the whole time. *Princess, what are you doing now?*

The lateness of the night took him to his last stop before bed, his study.

> *Love is real, real is love / Love is wanting to be loved*
> *Love is you / You and me*
> *Love is knowing / You can be.*

The old John Lennon record spun on a turntable, right next to the desk that was covered with sheets of paper.

> *Princess,*
> *Come back to our castle,*
> *our private universe that could shatter the Earth*
> *if only we could break open the wall*
> *and release a little piece of our souls.*
> *The sky is a window to vast galaxies,*
> *filled with untold mysteries.*
> *My window is these pieces of paper*
> *which hold all the questions my heart can't answer.*

The Earth makes our hearts tremble with its black,
untouched abysses.
I only have a black disk filled with songs,
a sea of words surrounded by melodies
and covered with memories.
Within this sea I will live and die
like a fish that spends its life cherishing the ocean,
then surrendering to its depths.
The world is a large coil wound around you and me.
All of this... For just you and me.

Ferré's first letter to Rana. No one knew that the letter existed, not Rafael, not even Rana herself. But that didn't matter. What mattered was that he had made contact with his own soul. For the first time he understood his path in this mortal life. It was the path leading to her.

I miss you. I miss your doubt. I miss your skepticism.
You are the one I chose.

And now, hour after hour, Ferré remembered that particular day, striving to commit it to memory, studying the chain of events that led them to today.

He was grateful he had accepted the request for an interview, otherwise... Grateful he had nothing scheduled that particular morning, otherwise... Grateful he was in his office, otherwise... Grateful to be alive, otherwise...

Everything begins with one movement.
Everything begins from a single idea.
Everything begins from a single choice.

Ferré never liked being interviewed. Scores of magazines and newspapers wanted to run stories about him. He was a great success, at least by conventional standards; although he had only recently turned twenty-nine, he was already a managing director. First it was the business magazines. Later the women's magazines wanted to make him their man of the month. Many agencies wanted to use him as a model in their ad campaigns. Even crazier, as far as Ferré was concerned, some production houses had offered him roles in television serials. Obviously they had no idea of the life a managing director in a multinational company led.

A lot of people thought of him as a jetsetter, surrounded by beautiful women and spending all of his time at wild parties. The difference between what they imagined and the reality of his life was vast.

It was true that he was used to the best of everything. His company car cost hundreds of million of rupiah! He flew first class and stayed in five-star hotels. But he passed through this world of luxury as if it were a dream. There were too many faxes to read, reports to study, telephone calls from all over the world to answer. With so much to think about, there wasn't time to enjoy the scenery.

Ferré was indeed surrounded by beautiful women. Dozens of them had offered themselves to him but he had only politely acknowledged them. Sometimes he simply stared. Time was too valuable to be used for anything but work.

There were wild parties. He had gone to a lot of them but always left before they became truly wild because he needed his strength for work the next day.

Quite inexplicitly, the day he first met Rana had been different from every other day: the first three hours in his appointment book were empty.

"Irma," he asked his secretary, "are you sure that I don't have anything scheduled this morning?"

"Quite sure, sir. Nothing at all."

Ferré mindlessly tapped his pen against his desk and his shoes against the floor. There were few phone calls, even fewer e-mails, and only a couple of reports to read. For no good reason, he went to the window and opened it slightly.

Irma's voice on the speakerphone interrupted his reverie: "Some new magazine wants to interview you, sir. They've asked if you're available."

"They never learn, do they," Ferré grumbled, but to his amazement, he didn't reject the request outright. He was more interested in a butterfly outside the window. Why should a beautiful white butterfly be hovering near this skyscraper?

"What kind of magazine?"

"A woman's magazine."

Spontaneously, he laughed.

"They brought by a copy of the magazine yesterday. It should be on your desk."

He leafed through the pile at the far left of his desk. "Oh, yes. I've found it." He opened the magazine briefly. It was boring. "Irma…"

His refusal hung suspended in midair. His attention shifted to the white butterfly, which now had flown into his office. The butterfly danced through the air and landed on his desk. Near the magazine. Suddenly Ferré noticed the magazine's logo: a butterfly.

Ferré was startled by Irma's voice. "Should I tell them not to bother, sir?"

"Wait a minute, wait a minute." Ferré realized that he was about to follow a hunch. "Tell them that I'll do it but…"

The butterfly flew into the air, circled, then found its way out the window. He was startled a second time.

"But what, sir?"

His brain resumed its normal programming. "But it has to be within the next three hours. After that, I'm out of here. If they can't come this morning, they can forget the whole thing."

A hunch. It had been many years since he had last used his intuition to make a decision. His mind was as sharp and as precise as a Pentium processor and no processor has any place for intuition.

Less than two hours later, a woman rushed into his office. She was breathing heavily.

"I'm not too late, am I?" she asked Ferré's secretary with panic in her voice. Although she was well aware of the stature of the man she was about to interview, she had not planned her interview and had no idea where the conversation might lead.

Irma opened the door: "Please go in."

The woman made an enormous effort to appear calm. To her surprise, the man immediately glanced at his watch.

"Good afternoon. You have one hour and ten minutes. I'm Ferré." He shook hands with her.

"I'm Rana," she replied. Her voice quivered. Slowly she set out her equipment: a notebook, ballpoint pen and a cassette recorder. Summoning her courage, she took a quick look at him. He was even more handsome than she had been told and, just as obviously, his own almost-mythical status was of no importance to him. People talked about him and not only in the business world. In the health clubs. At social gatherings. The masses were fascinated by him. Rana, too, had long been fascinated by him.

"Are we waiting for something?"

Utterly confused, Rana sighed several times. She didn't know where to begin. It was so embarrassing.

"Do you mind if I ask how old you are?"

Rana frowned. Her subject had asked the first question. "Twenty-eight. Why?"

Ferré laughed, the type of laugh that he should have stifled but couldn't. "I'm sorry. Forgive me. I was expecting someone older, a senior reporter, maybe; someone between thirty-five and forty."

"I'm the deputy editor," Rana quipped. "I've worked hard, the same as you. In a different field, that's all." It was a simple, honest response. Her body relaxed. Her voice became firm, confident. She looked directly at him. "To be honest, your conditions for the interview didn't give much me time to prepare. I've only the standard list of questions. Or if you'd prefer, we can just pick something out of the air."

"The air?" Ferré turned his chair toward her. He was suddenly interested.

"I mean we can start anywhere we feel like. Sometimes it's more fun to talk without really knowing where you're heading."

"You're right." Ferré smiled. "Tell me, what sort of an article do you want?"

"You probably won't be very interested. The column is called 'Daydreams.' Lots of women imagine all sorts of things about men like you. And we give them something to build their dreams on. Bring them closer to their fantasies. That's all."

"Oh. Here we are in the midst of an economic crisis and all your magazine can do is to encourage people to daydream."

Her attractive features hardened. "Are you too busy to daydream?" she countered.

"I never daydream, thank God."

"People don't only dream when they're asleep. Dreaming is a form of creativity. It can happen at any time. Some jobs make space for it. People who don't make time in their life for their dreams are robots."

Ferré found her vivaciousness irritating but his expression remained impassive.

"Was that your first question?"

Rana was silent for a moment. She was sorry she had spoken so directly.

"Why the butterfly?" Ferré asked again.

"I beg your pardon?" Again he had caught her by surprise. She began to wonder who was interviewing whom. She had not even turned on her tape recorder. Despite his charming appearance, he could be very annoying.

"Your magazine's logo. Why the butterfly?"

Rana wasn't quite sure of the answer to his question. "Perhaps the butterfly is a symbol of transformation. Or… people often think of the butterfly as a sign that a guest is coming and I want them to treat the magazine as a welcome guest in their homes."

"A butterfly visited me this morning. Here, in this skyscraper. Can you believe that? It simply came in through the window."

"Maybe it was telling you that I was coming. A large butterfly, wearing a white blouse." Rana smiled as she tugged at the hem of her blouse.

"How strange, you're right: it was a white butterfly," Ferré mumbled. He was too sophisticated to call it a coincidence. "And I guess you chose the name of the column as well."

"I did. How did you know?" Rana was impressed.

"You've only been here ten minutes but I already feel that I've known you for a long time. You know what you want. I like that." He smiled.

The warmth of his smile made something within Rana melt. She started to feel comfortable in the presence of this mythical being.

"OK. Let's start from the beginning." Rana switched on the tape recorder. "Your home and family. What influence did your parents have on you and your career?"

"My mother died when I was five. I never met my father. My grandparents raised me. They both died when I was eleven. In their will, they provided for me to be raised by friends of my grandfather living in San Francisco. The will covered my education right through college. My grandfather really took good care of everything, wouldn't you say?" Ferré sighed briefly. "So I guess that if anyone had an influence over me, it would have been my grandparents. And Gregory Tanner, a friend of my grandfather's, who came to be like a father to me."

The expression on his face was completely impassive. It was as if the dramatic events of his childhood had made absolutely no impression on him. Rana was amazed. The only other person she knew who could maintain such an expression was Mr Bean, as he drove his Mini Minor to work.

"Ferré?" she asked, cautiously using his name. "What did you want to be when you were a boy? A doctor? An engineer? The president?"

The man laughed. Most of the boys at his elementary school wanted to be one of those things.

"What about you, Rana?"

"A film star," she replied with a wry smile. "You?"

She doesn't realize how difficult that question is. It forced him back into the small dark cave of his childhood, which was filled with mud and slime. The muck that clogged his subconscious. No wonder Freud is so popular. Nothing is more interesting than watching a man drowning in the swamp of his own being.

His aim in life had been a real discovery for him, one he had found when working his way through his grandfather's bookshelves. There he found a few pages from an old comic book with a picture of a knight and a princess.

A Knight fell in love with a young Princess who lived in the land of the fairies. But one day the Princess returned to her home in the sky. The Knight was startled. He knew how to ride a horse and how to fight with his sword, but he didn't know how to fly.

The Knight left his castle and asked the butterflies to teach him to fly. But the butterflies could only teach him to fly to the top of the trees. So the Knight asked the sparrows to teach him to fly. They could only teach him to fly to the top of the church steeple. So he asked the eagles to teach him to fly. They could only take him to the top of the mountains. There was no winged creature that could teach him to fly any higher than that.

The Knight was sad, but he didn't give up. He asked the wind to teach him to fly. The wind taught him to fly around the world, to fly over the mountains and above the clouds. But the Princess was still much higher in the sky. The Knight despaired and this time he did give up hope.

One night a Falling Star heard him crying. The Star stopped and offered to teach him to travel at the speed of light. To travel faster than lightning and to fly higher than a million heavens. But if the Knight couldn't land right in front of the Princess, he would surely die. The dangerous speed at which he would be travelling would smash him into a fine red powder, and that would be the end of him. The Knight agreed. He was prepared to trust his life to the Falling Star. And he was ready to surrender his soul to a split second in time.

The Falling Star took his hand and whispered: "This is a journey of True Love. Close your eyes, oh noble Knight, and tell me to stop as soon as you feel that you are in the presence of the Princess."

They sped through the sky. The cold air seemed to tear the handsome Knight's heart to pieces, but his soul was warmed by his love for the Princess. And when he finally felt that she was near, he shouted: "Stop!"

The Falling Star looked down and was stunned by the beauty of the lonely Princess. The Princess shone like Andromeda in the darkness of outer space.

The Star fell in love with the Princess and let go of the Knight's hand, the Knight who was built from love and trust.

The Knight sped through space toward his own destruction. The Star landed and claimed the Princess.

The poor Knight.... But as a reward, he became the Aurora, red, blue and green swirls of light in the northern sky, a symbol to this very day of his faithfulness and sacrifice.

A bitterness the young Ferré could not explain made his eyes glaze over. For the first time in his life he had wept for a reason other than merely falling off his bicycle or out of the rose-apple tree; for a reason other than being bitten by a dog or stung by ants.

That night he had babbled to his grandmother about how unfair the story was. The Knight's faithfulness was surely worth more than the aurora borealis. What was the aurora anyway, Oma? Was it really pretty, Oma?

His grandmother tried to console him: "It is only a story, Ferré, a sad story. There are lots of other stories with happy endings." Unfortunately Ferré didn't believe her and his grandmother was forced to tell him dozens of stories, one after the other, all with happy endings, well into the night.

It was hard to comfort him. He wanted to know if there was any story sadder than that about the Knight, the Princess and the Falling Star. There wasn't. Or at least his grandmother didn't know any. Nor did his grandfather.

The story of the lead soldier who fell in love with the ballerina? No, they really did love each other. No one betrayed anyone else in that story. The soldier fell into the fire because he lost his balance. The mermaid who turned into froth? No, she was caught by her own curse.

In a childish voice Ferré said softly, "I want to be a knight, Oma." But when his grandmother asked him why, he couldn't explain. He was still too young to be able to explain what he really wanted: He wanted to turn the story around, to make the Falling Star vanish into a black hole. He wanted the Princess to realize that the Knight was a good man; that he had left his peaceful palace in order to learn to fly; that he was prepared to risk his life just to find her again.

Couldn't anybody else see it? That honesty had been taken for stupidity? That grand desires could have fatal consequences if one hadn't properly prepared oneself? That blind trust in another could be turned against the innocent? Plan everything thoroughly. Trust nobody but yourself. These were the lessons he had learned early in life.

He knew all this at that moment, without being able to put any of it into words.

His grandmother stroked his head. "You're only ten years-old, Ferré. You're still too young to be a knight. One day you will be, when you've grown up."

Less than a year later, his grandmother passed away. His grandfather followed her the next year. The white-haired angels who had nursed him and raised him, taught him how to read and add, who had read him stories and shown him how to pray.

Ferré blamed himself for their deaths. God must have heard him make that declaration. For years he had bothered his grandparents with his endless questions and his demands for new stories. Now he had to write his own story.

No. He hadn't wanted to be an engineer or a pilot or the president. There was only one thing he wanted and still wanted: to be a knight. He wanted the same story with a different ending. Not be tricked by love or by depending on someone else. He would learn to fly all by himself. Everything begins with a single choice.

Rana broke the unnaturally long silence. "I'm sorry. What did you want to be when you were a boy?" she carefully repeated.

Ferré looked up. Her face encouraged him to be honest. He wasn't sure why. People say that you can never tell whom you'll meet, or when. And today he had met someone who had forced him back into his childhood. Life is strange; so clear and yet so complicated.

"I wanted to be… a knight," he replied slowly, realizing how far he still was from his goal.

"Like an officer in the army, is that what you mean? Or a black-belt in judo?"

"That sort of thing."

Rana shook her head. "That's an unusual answer."

"It was an unusual question."

Rana looked at him. Their eyes met for only a few seconds but the experience was incredibly intense.

An acoustic piano begins to play in the background.

Rana didn't know what to do next. Although she didn't realize it, she wasn't alone in her confusion.

"You do have time for lunch, don't you?," Ferré asked.

Two violins swell the chorus.

Rana nodded. It had all happened so quickly. *There wasn't time to hide; not even the simple band of gold on her ring finger.*

Ferré noticed the ring later at lunch. "Are you married?"

"Yes," Rana vaguely replied.

"How long?"

"Three years."

"You got married when you were twenty-five? That's pretty young by today's standards. Any special reason?"

"My parents. His parents, even more. They thought we'd be better off getting married than misbehaving ourselves. I'd finished university and had a job, so there was no reason to wait."

Ferré blinked in disbelief. "It's the first time I've heard that excuse."

"For someone who spent his youth studying in San Francisco it probably is a little unusual."

Rana didn't tell him how much in love she had been: in love with the idea of being married, of having her own home and her own husband. A young couple, with a house in some new real-estate development, sharing a credit card, holding hands as they pushed a cart around the supermarket, discussing which brand of detergent to buy, what sort of instant noodle, which company made the best chili sauce.

"What is it like being married? Is it nice?" He glanced at Rana. He could tell instantly she was a bad liar. There was something she wanted to keep from him. "It's OK," she said, trying to appear casual. "It's fine. Not exactly what I expected, but not too bad."

"Sorry. It's not my place to ask that sort of thing. But I'm always impressed by the way people can make a serious commitment because they're in love. I've never even had a serious relationship."

"You mean you've never had time for one?"

"Exactly! That's precisely it." Ferré laughed.

"As bad as that?"

His laughter vanished. "Is that bad?" he asked seriously.

"Isn't it?" Rana replied in amazement. "You lead a stressful life. Surely you need someone to help you relax? Wouldn't you like someone who could cook your meals, go to the movies with you, take walks, go shopping…."

"Hold on, hold on," Ferré interrupted. "One thing at a time. Firstly, I don't like to go shopping. Next, if I ever want to go for a walk or watch a movie, I have lots of friends I can ask to come with me. My housekeeper is a fantastic cook, even if I must admit that I eat out more often than I eat at home. And I think I'm quite capable of relaxing on my own. But, all right, if there was someone who could do all those things, I could be tempted." He smiled. "Is that why you got married, Rana? Because you found the total package?"

"I suppose so…" Her voice drifted off, like a helium balloon running out of gas.

"But it wasn't what you expected?"

Rana sighed. "Things happen. You should expect them, but you don't. That's where commitment comes in."

"Commitment makes up for a lot of things."

Rana wasn't enjoying the conversation.

"Perhaps that is one reason I never wanted a serious relationship," Ferré said lightly. "When I meet someone at work half way, there is always a pay-off. But I refuse to compromise in my personal life. A half-hearted relationship is worthless."

"Sometimes you need to make sacrifices," Rana said wearily.

"Then which idiot said, 'Love will set you free'? I thought love was a ticket to freedom, not to sacrificing yourself. Maybe I'm too idealistic."

Neither of them said anything for a long time. Too long, in fact. Their silence spoke volumes.

"It has been a very interesting interview. Thank you." Rana rose to leave. "I'll send you a copy of the article."

"Do you have a business card?"

"I'm sorry I forgot to bring one, but hold on a moment." Rana tore a leaf from her notepad and wrote the number of her cellphone on it.

Ferré wrote his personal number on his business card. "Here, this is mine."

Rana was delighted.

The piano begins playing again, a very light and happy tune.

"Rana?"

The young woman turned. Her eyes shone. Ferré was captivated by her eyes. They were the eyes of a person who could overcome the fiercest challenge in order to fulfill every dream. They were like his own.

"Are you the baby of the family?"

"How did you know?"

Ferré smiled slightly and shrugged his shoulders.

Little princess from the Kingdom of Fairies,
I never thought I'd meet you so soon.

The violins play again.

Ferré could still hear the background music but it sounded different now. Still beautiful, to be sure, yet somehow tinged with melancholy.

He wanted to sleep.

3

Unexpected Turbulence

"I don't get it," Dhimas said, looking at his notes. "A man like the Knight could have anyone he wants. So when he falls in love, the woman should be truly extraordinary. That woman you've described is so undistinguished. I mean, OK, she's a career woman, a graduate of a top school, and not bad looking either, but none of that tells me that there is anything special about her."

"That's exactly the point," Ruben replied. "The mystery of love. The heart recognizes qualities the mind cannot see. Ferré sees something no one else can."

"What does he see? I can tell you her whole life in one breath: first she's born; then she goes to kindergarten, elementary school, high school, college; gets a job, gets married, has a few kids, some grandchildren, too, until, finally, she dies and becomes food for worms. It is all so predictable. Where is the excitement in that?"

"The quantum leap, Mr Freud! Ring any bell?" Ruben shouted impatiently. "You see, we need her predictability. We need someone boring. Imagine her like a machine with a screw loose that's ready to pop out and ruin the whole system. An unexpected turbulence."

"A what?"

"If only you could imagine how complex human thought is," Ruben said, rolling his eyes upwards. "So complex that the mirror can flip over at any moment. Order, chaos: as easy as turning your hand. The human mind continually hovers at a spot prior to the point of bifurcation. With one brief moment of turbulence—the consequence of one unstable act after another—our character can find herself at that critical moment where absolutely anything can happen."

Dhimas began to understand what Ruben was driving at. "The unnoticed instability, I like that," he said as he chewed on the end of his ballpoint. "An abstract problem, so abstract that nobody notices it. But absolutely essential. And with enormous consequences when sufficiently magnified."

"You sound just like me. Wonderful."

"Why would anyone want to be a clown like you?" Dhimas grumbled. "I still can't figure it out, though. A problem that is abstract and absolutely essential. Lurking somewhere in the corner of her life like a sleeping virus that's ready to strike."

Ruben grinned. "Come on. You know exactly what it is."

4

The Princess

With her head pressed against the window, she watched the cars pass. She read almost all the street names. Missed none of the billboards or banners. It was an old habit. Something she had always done and still did.

None of it meant anything to her now. When she was a girl, things had been different. Rana didn't know what had vanished. The same eyes, the same person, but now she saw things in a completely different way.

The car stopped.

"I'll pick you up at seven, OK?" asked Arwin, her husband.

"Sure. If there's any change, I'll call."

When the car drove away, Rana stood stock still, her feet planted on the pavement of the portico but her mind high in the sky, busily searching, wondering about her own limits. How much longer could she continue with this charade?

She felt a piercing jealousy of yesterday's Rana, the one who wasn't bothered by the monotony of her own life; the Rana with a heart of ice, not fire; the Rana who never asked any questions. Today, she had to struggle to make sense of a personal history that now seemed distant and strange:

Rana the New Graduate

After five years consuming technical scientific knowledge that was of absolutely no interest to her, Rana had fulfilled her filial obligations and met her parents' expectations. For five years, they had enjoyed their daughter's achievements: she had gained entrance to the Bandung Institute of Technology, one of Indonesia's most prestigious universities, where she had enrolled in one of the most demanding departments and excelled in her studies. Now she was free to do what she wanted. She turned to journalism, became a reporter, and spent her life going here and there and meeting all sorts of people. But now she realized this wasn't what she had wanted either. Her job was merely an escape and even the current Rana was a complete fraud.

Her mind kept rewinding.

Rana, Age Twenty

She met Arwin, a refined man from an aristocratic family, seven years her senior. Good background, well behaved, excellent prospects—all the admirable traits a prospective son-in-law was supposed to have—and her parents were immediately smitten. What a son-in-law he would be. What a family he came from. He had this and that, his relatives were this person and that, and his friends were well placed in this government department or that one. It was wonderful—at least in the beginning—and everyone told Rana over and over again how lucky she was to have a man like Arwin. Brainwashed, she repeated: "Yes, I am lucky," "Arwin is perfect, isn't he?" "Our families get on so well together," and "Why wait any longer?" They were married as soon as she finished university. The wedding was at the top of her agenda, with a planning checklist filled with superlatives. The lavish reception was held in the ballroom of one of Jakarta's top hotels whose facilities were first class, as were the wedding celebrants, the food and the entertainment. The cost ran into hundreds of millions of rupiah and the newlyweds received more than had been spent. All the right people came. Endless rolls of film were used to record the event: shots of family, groups of friends and Jakarta's socialites in special poses. But once the pictures were developed, she still hadn't been able to see what all the fuss had been about.

Perhaps she needed to step further back.

Rana as a Teenager

A happy and active teenage girl, a good friend and diligent student, she seldom caused any trouble, but…. Suddenly Rana's mind was spinning with questions she'd never explored before. Why did she need so much extra tutoring? Why was her mother on such good terms with her teachers, to the extent of giving them small envelopes each time she went to receive Rana's report cards? Why did she have to learn Balinese dancing? Why did she have to join the swimming club and have her father follow her up and down the pool, shouting at her, stopwatch in hand? Why did she have to get at least a B in all her science subjects, but no one complimented her when she got an A in Indonesian? Why did she have to major in science, just because her parents and their friends grew up in an era when engineering was the most prestigious profession? And why couldn't she ever go out with the boys she liked, just because her parents hadn't grown up with "that sort of fellow"? It was crazy. Rana was no longer a teenager, but she still couldn't answer any of those whys.

Her last hope was one step farther back...

Rana as a Child

Rana struggled to remember as far back as she could. One afternoon, playing in the broad yard behind her house, with her toys scattered over the grass. She heard her mother call out: "Rana! It's late. Take a bath and go with your sisters to their Quran class." And tiny Rana did as she was told. Dressed in a pink prayer veil, she happily followed her sisters to the house of the chanting instructor.

When they arrived, the teacher gave Rana a piece of paper and some colored pencils, thinking the child was too young to understand the Quran. And Rana didn't understand. All she heard was a song in a foreign language that was supposed to be a prayer. So she didn't chant. What she really wanted were the snacks served to the pupils half way through the class.

Unsettled, Rana spoke up. "Ma'am," she asked the pious instructor, "if I want to talk to God, how do I do it? I don't know how to pray in Arabic." The wise teacher had replied: "A small child like you can speak directly to God. He'll hear you." Rana was impressed. All the way home, she whispered: "God… God." She could see a scene from the old television comedy series "Mork and Mindy." Mork's face appears. He is cailing Orson. She hears Orson's booming reply: "Yes, Mork."

To her surprise, the voice was very soft. She could hardly hear it. But she was sure that there was a voice.

God was very funny and he often made Rana laugh. He was kind too. Once Rana yearned for a cone of bright pink cotton candy in a street vendor's cart but she didn't have any money. Suddenly, a father approached and bought one for his daughter. The seller didn't have any change, so the father bought two and gave one to Rana. She was overwhelmed with delight.

Rana was never lonely, she always had God to play with. He sent her squirrels scrambling down from the trees, puppies miraculously appeared in her front yard, birds landed unexpectedly on her head.

When she started to learn to read, God was her mentor. He spoke to her through the letters of the alphabet. Once she asked Him if she could have a Lego set as her birthday present. To her surprise, a truck appeared, with a yellow note painted on its rear panel: "From Mama." On the night before her birthday party, her mother had sneaked into her room and placed the Lego set right beside her bed. Rana realized that God spoke in many ways, through many people, in many different places. That was when she had started to sit silently in the car, reading all the signs as they passed. But then, gradually, the conversations ceased, the writing on the signs became merely writing, without any meaning. Routine had taken over.

By then, Rana had learned to chant the Quran. She had devoured it, working her way through from beginning to end many times. But she never heard that voice again. With each year, there was more there to think about: homework, after-school classes, her New Kids on the Block collection. There was no time to listen to the silence. The voices all around her demanded that she pay attention to them. And now she was…

Rana Standing in the Portico

At last she now knew what had vanished but she still didn't know how to get it back.

An empty feeling hung over the dining table. Perhaps it was because there were only the two of them living in the large house. Or perhaps it was the gap they had deliberately created between themselves.

Arwin looked at his wife as she bent over her plate and waited for the right moment to speak to her.

"Rana," he called softly.

"Yes?" she replied in the same voice.

"You're so quiet these days. Is something wrong? Can I do anything to help?"

Rana bowed her head deeper. *There is something wrong. I've fallen in love with another man. Can we go back a few years and not get married?*

"I want you to tell me if I've done anything wrong," he said even more softly. "It's important we communicate honestly with each other."

"You haven't done anything wrong, Arwin." *Apart from that one thing.*

"Are you well? When was the last time you had a check-up?"

Rana had been born with a defective valve in her heart. Because of the added complication of an atrial staple defect, she had undergone her first operation at the age of ten. Ever since then, she had had a regular examination every six months. Arwin worried about her health. He hoped that one day she would be able to bear children. At any rate, they had decided to have a baby during the coming year.

"I'm fine. A bit tired."

"You've been working too hard. You seem to be out every night, at one event or another. You should learn to delegate a bit; there are other people in your office, you know."

"Thanks for the advice," she said sincerely. *My schedule is starting to look a little unusual, isn't it? I must try not to be so obvious.*

"Mom called me at work today. She's planning a family gathering at the country house this Saturday. Let's go, OK? Your folks are invited too."

Automatically, Rana looked away. *I'm tired of forcing myself to smile all day. I'm bored of them asking me when they can play with their grandchild. Bored of the same old charade, year in year out. I'm bored. Bored, bored, bored!*

"What's wrong?" he asked, trying to interpret her expression. "Do you have to work?"

Hesitantly, she nodded. *I just want to vanish for one whole day. Ferré is free all Saturday.*

"Come on, Rana. We don't see them very often. Make some time now and then. You shouldn't be on stand-by for your office 24-7."

"I'll check my schedule."

The dining table disappeared into a whirlpool. Rana was flooded by feelings of reluctance. Arwin drowned in a multitude of questions. Nothing floated to the surface.

5

The Great Question

R uben placed the draft of the story on the table and sipped at yet another cup of coffee. "The miserable wretches," he said with delight.

"Which part do you like best?" Dhimas asked.

"I like the part where the Princess is standing at the entry to her office building, reviewing her life. You've described her regression brilliantly. That is exactly how the process of bifurcation happens."

"Please explain."

"Feedback occurs when the system turns back on itself. The process is called a loop. There are two types of loops: negative loops stabilize the system, positive loops amplify it. When the Princess was a girl, her system was amplified. As she grew older, her environment placed increasing pressure on her and a negative loop developed. So her life has been stable for a long time. However, her love for the Knight creates a positive loop, which will amplify everything once again. And what will the result be? An enormous storm. All the order she has worked to maintain all this time is only a hairsbreadth away from total collapse!" Ruben laughed triumphantly.

Dhimas scratched his head. "Sometimes I'm not sure which one of us is crazy: you, for mixing your television soap opera with your weird scientific theories, or me, for writing them down."

"We're both mad, you know that."

"Thanks for reminding me."

"I also liked it when the Knight was remembering that story from his childhood: what a neat description of exactly the same process. But I still can't figure out how you manage to bring those two dimensions together: the soul of a poet, buried in the body of a young executive? What a bizarre concept."

Without saying a word, Dhimas took an old comic book from his briefcase. Despite its faded cover, the title of the comic was still visible: *The Knight, the Princess and the Falling Star.*

Ruben was stunned. "There really is such a book! It does exist!"

"The impact it made on me wasn't quite as dramatic as the influence it had over the Knight but it did start me off on the path to being a poet. You must read it, Ruben. It is the most poetic kid's book imaginable."

"Sure, sure," Ruben interrupted. "But at the moment I'm more interested in the book you're writing now."

"Whatever." Offended, Dhimas grimaced.

Ruben was too caught in his own thoughts to notice the look on Dhimas' face. With increasing fervor he explained: "Both moments you have so beautifully described are the exact moments when they finally recognize the strange attractor!"

"Again explain," Dhimas said curtly.

"First things first: attractors are creatures that live in a curious abstract space known as phase space."

"Phase space?" Dhimas repeated emphatically.

Ruben clicked his tongue in annoyance. "OK. Phase space is an imaginary map of the way a particular thing can move. It can include as many dimensions and variables as are required to describe that motion. These can be calculated with reference to either the position or the velocity of the object."

"For example?"

"Oh, this is so tedious," Ruben sighed. "Take a map of the journey between Jakarta and Surabaya, for example. A bus driver could tell you every twist and turn of the road, from start to end, just from memory. But his map wouldn't be any use to a pilot. The pilot needs a completely different map. Phase space charts every possible alternative, including those small but critical turning points which could send you off to Yogyakarta instead of Surabaya. By using phase space to chart the way in which a system moves we can discover how a previously orderly system can suddenly turn into chaos and vice versa. Does that make sense?"

"Let's go back to the handsome stranger; or is it the strange attractor?"

"Strange attractor. Keep your mind on the job. It is...." Suddenly Ruben stopped. An image flashed in his mind, like a television commercial. The most beautiful picture he had ever seen: a picture of Mandelbrot fractal space voyage.

When modern scientists began to realize their predecessors' shortcomings and started to pay attention to areas outside those usually observed, they found fractals. Wherever chaos, turbulence and disorder are found, fractal geometry is at play. A strange attractor is a fractal curve. Fractal shapes are the same as descending scales. For systems under the folding and stretching influence of the strange attractor, any single folding of motion of the system represents a mirror of the entire folding operation. These strange attractors organize the whole system and, at the same time, bear the mode of its disorganization. They are called "strange" because even though they are disorganized, they help the system stay organized. All of life, at every level, is full of fractals, from the material level to pure energy, from the physical to the mental. They are the foundation of everything and they are characterized by their complete inability to sustain anything at all.

Ruben still remembered how amazed he had been when he first saw a Mandelbrot fractal voyage picture on the cover of a *Scientific American* belonging to one of his professors. A Mandelbrot set is a formula, believed to be the most complicated in the realm of mathematics. The formula is based on only two variables: C, which is a fixed number, and Z, which is a complex number allowed to vary. Inputting this $Z^2 + C$ equation into a computer will produce a mathematical cosmos and send the explorer of the Mandelbrot set off on an infinite voyage.

In the beginning, the set looked fairly straightforward. A molecule made of bonded atoms, one with a cardioid shape, the other nearly circular. But once mathematicians studied the picture in greater detail, enlarging it billions of times, something extraordinary happened. Within that simple shape, there were a zillion mind-boggling points where the design branched out infinitely, and they were all—amazingly—exact reproductions of the original geometrical shape. This happened even when the scale was as small as a nano. The first shape, the mother set, which is the strange attractor, was like some stubborn, enduring memory.

"I'm still waiting," Dhimas repeated.

"A strange attractor is…" Ruben paused, then emphasized: "…a question."

"A question?"

"Have you ever felt that we are all born into this world with one great question? This question is concealed in every cell of our bodies. It haunts us. We are continually driven by it. It is as though the one true mission of our lives is to find an answer to this question."

"Yes, well?" Dhimas could still not see the relevance of Ruben's remarks.

"The question hangs over every single atom in the whole of existence. It isn't a question only for the human species. It is expressed in countless different ways: changes in the weather; earthquakes; the appearance of new forms of flora and fauna; the way the sun rises and sets. They are all driven by the same question.

No matter where we turn, or how far we run, we cannot escape it. Do you know something, Dhimas? My gut tells me that this question is the one basic substance that unites us all and everything in the universe."

"But, but, what is the question?"

"*Who am I?*"

6

Reversed Order Mechanism

The room was filled with stacks of papers and mountains of books. The PC hummed softly. As the modem flickered, two hands typed unceasingly at the keyboard.

Sometimes the hands could type for hours on end, day after day. Speed was essential. There was so much to write; too much, in fact: an article a week, hundreds of questions to answer each night. The inbox was always almost completely full, just an e-mail away from total capacity. How wonderful it would be to have as many hands as an octopus had legs.

Late at night, the final letter flashed across the screen:

> Sometimes, Supernova, when I'm really sick and tired of this living death, I think of killing myself. Finish everything. Maybe when I'm dead I'll understand what life is all about. Why aren't people allowed to kill themselves?
>
> What's wrong with it?
>
> I'm in total awe of people who decide to take their own lives. They don't die in an accident or because they're sick or someone kills them. They do it themselves.

Supernova, who do you think was the greatest person in the twentieth century?

Of all the possibilities, I nominate Kurt Cobain.

Yeah, now he really was a product of Generation X. After a brief smile, the hands began typing a reply.

>Maybe by really dying I will discover the meaning of life.

Don't you want to find out the meaning of life when you are still alive? That would be true happiness.

>Supernova, who do you think was the greatest person in the twentieth century?

Albert Einstein. He discovered the concept which made your Kurt Cobain's suicide neither true nor false.

<send>

In the phosphorescent light of the monitor, two eyes shone brightly. Thoughts flashed at a speed making the RAM of any computer seem like a dying snail.

Dhimas and Ruben

Ruben sat in the same chair, with the pile of books beside him growing ever higher. Dhimas worked with all his might at his laptop. Although they seemed to be travelling through different worlds they were clearly wrestling with the same problem.

"Ruben, about our other character...."

"That's funny, I was thinking the same thing."

"The Falling Star...."

"I thought you meant the Dragon."

Dhimas snorted. His lover had such a crap visual imagination. "Sorry to disappoint you, Ruben, but I just can't write about a character covered in scales blowing fire out of his nose."

"Falling Star. Hmm. I like the sound of that."

"How do you see this character?"

"Someone who represents the gray area: the theory of relativity on legs, full of paradoxes, neither an antagonist nor a protagonist."

"A meteor flashing across all of our skies, who overwhelms us, then completely vanishes."

"Not constrained by any institution or any organization, belonging to no one."

"A man or..."

"A woman?"

Both men fell silent.

"The Falling Star stole the Princess," Dhimas mumbled, "so it ought to be a man, if we were going to follow the original story. But when the point of bifurcation happened during his childhood, the Knight wanted to rewrite the whole story anyway."

"By not letting himself be tricked by the lustful Falling Star, right? He wanted to win the Princess for himself so that they could live happily after. Done!"

"You disappoint me," Dhimas sighed. "We should forget those old concepts of revenge: an eye for an eye, a tooth for a tooth. That sort of thing only leads to more misery. It's as old fashioned as your simple reductionists."

On hearing the term "reductionist," Ruben stopped talking. He refused to be considered one of *them*.

"Let's show our readers how the Knight evolves emotionally. What he once thought meant the world to him is actually just one among an infinity of options. And finally his emotional responses lead him to true maturity, not to revenge. To true compassion."

"That's a tough one," Ruben said, sorting through various theories.

"So, our Falling Star has to be a woman."

"A different sort of woman, one who is almost totally impersonal."

"That's hard."

"You tell me."

They were both silent again.

"Hey, do you remember what Abraham Maslow said?" Ruben exclaimed.

Dhimas' eyes widened. "Obviously, no, but I bet you do, hey?"

"When human beings have satisfied their basic needs, then they can begin the search for something beyond mere survival. They can work on self actualization, knowledge of the self at the deepest level. That is the level she should already have achieved."

"Which means she has to be rich, so that she doesn't have to worry about daily survival. She has to be beautiful, so the body isn't of concern to her. She has to be well educated and blessed with a superior mind, so that intellectually she isn't trapped at the material and physical levels. But she mustn't be bound by any institution or organization. What can we make her? An entrepreneur?"

"Sort of. She needs the sort of position that provides her with the maximum degree of independence and freedom. Do you know what I mean?"

"I'm not sure I do."

"If she were a politician, she would have to choose one side or another when she talked about politics. If she were a scholar or an intellectual, everything she said would have to start from her discipline. A merchant is always thinking about profit and loss. A religious figure has to defend certain dogmas. We need someone who is an absolute observer, with no pretensions to being anything else. Not a saint, and certainly not an ascetic, because people like that rarely enjoy all that life has to offer."

"A prostitute!"

"A what?" Ruben leaped out of his chair.

"Listen to me. When a person achieves the freedom of thought which self actualization implies, their ideas can neither be bought nor sold. The only thing they can sell is their body. And a prostitute is a sort of a business woman. We'll make her free of all ties, so fantastic she won't even need a pimp!"

"But that's a paradox. If she is so smart, how can she degrade herself to become a prostitute?"

"She's precisely the paradoxical sort of human being you want!" Dhimas shouted triumphantly. "You mustn't look at her the way everyone else does. Don't judge her by the simple opposites of good and evil. Try to think what sort of a person she would be, Ruben, living on both sides of the mirror at the same time, a life of utter relativity. Can you imagine the process of bifurcation she must have been through? How intense the process of amplification must have been to have led to the destruction of her entire system?"

Ruben shook his head. "You're speaking my language, but I can't even begin to imagine her."

"Then try the 'reversed order mechanism.'"

It was a like a cue call. "Yes, you're right, Dhimas," Ruben said slowly, his eyes dancing. "You're absolutely right!"

"When we reverse our perspective by one hundred and eighty degrees, then the truth is reversed as well. There are prostitutes everywhere. Almost all of us constantly prostitute ourselves in one way or another: we sell our time, our dignity, our thinking, even our souls. And aren't those the worst forms of prostitution of all?"

7

The Falling Star

The stage was decorated in silver. Everyone was infected with the excitement of the approaching new millennium. Mysterious strains of ambient music began to fill the air. The notes hung on each atom, gestured toward some imaginary world, and followed each woman as she made her entrance.

The tall bodies were all the same. High up on the stage, the models were thin, some as thin as bread sticks. When they walked they swayed so vigorously that it seemed they might snap at the waist at any moment. Their eyes stared menacingly into the dark room in front of them.

One model stood out. The difference was no simple matter: it had to do with her eyes. Her gaze was not merely sharp; it seemed to cut like a sword through those on whom it fell. The others were like a shining row of knives, blunt knives. Her eyes did not stare into empty space, but sought to engage with every eye watching her. She stripped the audience bare. The confrontation pleased her much more than the act of parading before them.

Entrance after entrance, she was the one they waited for. They all knew that. They offered themselves to her for her eyes to do with them as she would.

Her last appearance. She vanished behind the stage.

"Diva…"

The young woman turned around.

"Frans wants you to go on stage with him," said Adi, the stage manager.

"Why not Nia?"

"Frans changed his mind."

"At the last minute?"

Adi nodded. "At the last minute." He was used to her ways. Maybe no one had ever liked Diva. People said she was bitter. Not friendly, not distant, but cold; cold in a very unpleasant way. There was a cruel edge to her tongue, which she made no attempt to conceal. But she was also like a magnet and could bring even the most resistant elements to her side sooner or later.

Diva drove a hard bargain. She was a top model. The goods she advertised belonged to the very top end of the market. Her appearances were reserved for the best shows and the most exclusive magazines. She commanded the highest rates and never did anything for free. But she was a true professional, as easy to mold as plastic polymer. She never complained and was always on time.

That night the other models watched as she walked to the front of the stage with the designer. Their expressions ranged from surprise to pure jealousy.

To be honest, she never really liked these kinds of places.

There was nothing friendly about the cruel looks which crawled over her body and devoured her long legs. The people were like wild animals that spent day after day chained in a narrow cage and now had been released to watch the show. They didn't know how to handle their freedom.

Waves of perverted thoughts hung obscenely in the air. Diva felt stifled, but she was too bored to care. Slinging her large bag over her shoulder, she pushed her way through the swaying crowd of people, a wild fire waiting to consume her.

"Diva!" shouted her agent, as she ran after Diva with a tote bag in her hand. "Your shoes! You're unbelievably forgetful."

"*Merci*." Diva took the bag in such a way that she seemed deliberately not to take it at all, just to watch Risty catch her breath.

"You can pick up your fee tomorrow at lunch time. OK?"

"Sure."

"How are you getting home?"

Diva shrugged. "I'll take a taxi, I guess. My driver is sick and I couldn't be bothered driving myself."

"Do you want me to drop you off?" Risty offered, hoping Diva wouldn't accept. It was hard work being with her for any length of time. "If you do, I hope you won't mind waiting around while I finalize a few things backstage first."

"Don't worry. I'm already on my way out." Diva smiled and turned to leave.

"Diva!" Risty called again. "Don't forget the program tomorrow afternoon, all right? Sorry, but that's a direct order from the top." Risty pointed upwards and, despite herself, smiled in a malicious, satisfied way.

Diva understood Risty's intention perfectly. She was an easy target for the stupid jobs her agency set up, like being a member of a panel to judge a children's fashion parade. They exploited her but she didn't have the energy to protest.

As soon as she stepped out of the café, the alarm on her cellphone rang, reminding her of an appointment. Diva sighed. Risty was right: she was becoming hopelessly forgetful. Perhaps she needed better technology, a bookmark to separate the pages of time. To remind her of the trash she preferred not to remember but nevertheless still had to do.

Less than five minutes later, the phone rang. "Hello. Diva?" said a man's voice. "Are you ready? Where are you? I'll pick you up, OK? I'm on my way. Wait for me."

Fifteen minutes later, a jet-black, shiny sedan arrived.

"Hello, beautiful."

The greeting was accompanied by a broad grin. The grin belonged to Dahlan. A man in his early forties, at the height of his career, married to a woman he had dated in high school, the father of two kids. There was something he could not quite define missing in his life. Diva was one of the ways he had found to hide his emptiness.

"Hello," Diva briefly replied.

"How was the show? A success? You look incredibly beautiful. I'm glad I could catch up with you afterwards."

"The show? Yes, it was a success. Beautiful? Of course. I know that. Am I glad to see you? Probably not. To be honest, I'm exhausted. I'd even forgotten our appointment. But don't worry, I'm a professional." She drew her hair onto her head. Clipped it there. And fanned her neck.

Dahlan grew increasingly agitated and pushed the accelerator toward the floor.

"We're in luck, Div. My office had a function at the Hyatt today. And look what I've got," Dahlan waved a plastic room key at her.

"Bringing home garbage from your office is nothing to be proud of."

Dahlan laughed, impervious to her remarks. "I really want you, Diva. It is a pity your fee is so high."

"My rate is my safeguard. Imagine what would happen if I reduced my price. The sort of nonsense I'd have to put up with, from people just like you. The common people. The masses."

Dahlan laughed even more loudly. "Oh Diva, I love you!"

The springs of the luxurious mattress finally came to rest after the beating they had taken. For the next few hours the couple only talked.

Dressed in a white terry cloth gown, Diva took a bottle of mineral water from the mini bar. Dahlan lay back comfortably on the bed with the sheet wrapped around him from the waist down.

"Can you believe it," she said. "An automotive worker in Malaysia earns as much in a month as an automotive worker in Illinois earns in one day. One French worker earns as much as forty-seven Vietnamese workers. An American mechanic is equal to sixty Chinese mechanics. This is how we measure the worth of human beings these days. But you won't find it written up in any brochure in this hotel." Diva stopped her chatter to take another sip of water. "Advances in productivity all revolve around the same question: which is cheaper, machines or humans? And the answer is always the same, too: humans. So if a company considers establishing a factory in Japan, it always focuses on machines first because labor there is so expensive. But why would anyone rush to invest so much capital in machines? Such a decision could undermine a firm's competitive capacity before it even got going. In the end, the problem simply comes back to the question of which country can provide the cheapest labor. Political policy and personal loyalty both finish a poor second." She giggled. "Marx must be laughing in his grave."

"Are you telling me that the state institutions are only an accessory after the fact?"

"What I'm saying is that they are insignificant, but try telling them that! The point is, capitalism has created its own democratic forum. For the first time in history, sovereignty has passed from the state to transnational business. And don't forget the magic mantra: 'of the consumer, for the consumer, by the consumer'. But you're right, the state has to be seen by its ignorant citizens to have some role in the whole process. And not only are the citizens ignorant, they have to be kept ignorant for as long as possible."

"You don't like government officials, do you?" Dahlan commented. Then he added, half-teasingly: "Surely you must have some clients who are bureaucrats?"

"Lots of them, but if you think I don't like them, then you should realize that I don't care much for your crew either: multinational businessmen. To be frank, I'm not concerned at all with liking and not liking. We're all in our own line of business. I prefer to trade with the elite; you never give anything away for free and I don't intend to either. All you know is the language of money. And money can't write poetry."

"Bullshit! I can hire a poet to write me a poem any time I want. Anywhere."

"That's what I said. You're all the same. You think you can buy something that can't be sold. It's a delusion. Possessing someone's body doesn't mean that you own them."

"Diva, you're a sadist. Do you know that?"

"Answer me one thing, Dahlan. Are you a citizen of Indonesia or your company?"

"Indonesia, of course."

"Well, what have you ever done for Indonesia?"

"Quite a lot, really. I pay my taxes, provide new employment opportunities, introduce the latest technology, look after my staff...."

Diva looked at Dahlan and laughed. "Is that you or your German company talking?"

Dahlan did not answer.

"If the MNC you work for went bankrupt tomorrow and vanished from the face of the Earth, who would introduce the new technology then? Who are you really, Dahlan? Who?" Diva giggled. "Knock! Knock! Hello? Is anybody in there?"

Dahlan laughed with her. In fact, he laughed louder than Diva.

"'*Gleiche Arbeit, gleicher Lohn*', as your Helmut Kohl said. The same pay for the same work." Diva began gathering her clothes. "But that doesn't apply to me."

"What about you? Which country do you belong to, Diva darling?"

"I'm a child of nature. I do whatever I think is best at the time. In my book, the state, the nation and everything that goes with them all belong in a museum. And it would be naïve of me to think that life exists only in the world I can see with my own two eyes."

"So you believe in UFOs?"

"Don't get me wrong. I'm not talking about flying saucers and little green men!" she exclaimed. "I'm not concerned with the physical form. It's like the water in a ditch staring in amazement at the ocean, though they're both water. When I say life, I mean the very essence of life itself—vitality, energy—flowing through everything in all its purity. When that force is blocked, unable to move freely, it becomes dead and stagnant."

Dahlan frowned. "Sometimes I don't understand what you're talking about."

"Maybe you're too stubborn to make the effort."

"Diva," Dahlan murmured. "There are times when I think you're smarter than my CEO. I don't understand at all why you do this. With a mind like yours, you could have a much better position than I have."

The woman smiled at him mockingly. "I am smarter than either you or your CEO, which is why I don't want to work the way you do. Ultimately there isn't any difference between our various professions. As I've said before, we're both in business, we simply deal in different commodities. I'm not interested in what you have to sell. I'd rather be free to think what I want to think. And I have something unique to offer my customers."

"Is that why you charge in dollars?" Dahlan interrupted her, laughing. He reached for his briefcase, took out the envelope he had already prepared, and gave it to Diva.

"*Gleiche Arbeit, verschiedener Lohn*: the same work, different pay," she replied lightly. "That's my principle."

"Do you know something? I'd pay whatever you asked just to listen to you talk."

"Don't kid yourself. You enjoyed both parts of the evening's entertainment, didn't you?" Diva prepared to leave. "Time to go."

"Don't forget we have another appointment next week!"

"Do we?" Surprised, Diva checked the list of clients she had scanned into her cellphone. "You're right," she mumbled.

The woman departed, without paying the man any further attention.

Everything seemed to pass very quickly when one was in Diva's presence. It was as if she inhabited a different dimension of time and that she could drag everybody else into it with her. Now that she had left, Dahlan felt as though he had been flung back into a world where time moved in slow, ungainly spurts. Fortunately he could still dimly sense her vitality in the room: the energy of life itself.

In the taxi, Diva stared vacantly at the road around her. The city never rested. The pendulum of time drove it to work nonstop. Enormous hands, the same invisible hands that prodded people to rise from their beds and begin to work, swept through every corner of the capital. The same hands that would then drive them home again later, loaded down with worries and uneasy dreams. The same invisible hands that would smash anyone who dared to disobey its rhythm, who preferred a life of leisure. Adam Smith had seen those hands. His theories were now commonplace, taught in every school.

But sometimes Diva felt utterly alone, the only person who could really see the hands as they played cat-and-mouse with her.

Everyone else seemed to be extremely organized, utterly content to work like machines. And when the sun rose in the morning, they would still proudly claim to be human beings.

Diva sighed. She was tired. The world seemed so stale and weary, so over exploited. It spun endlessly on the same rusty axle and pretended that it was always evolving. There was nothing new. Every time someone laughed, they were trying to hide some old hurt. Every time they cried, they were preparing to laugh at someone else's expense.

Diva realized how hard it was to reach out and try to live. To resist death. To live among the corpses of those who had not yet realized that they had already died a long time ago.

Diva strode into the mall. As always on weekends, the noise was deafening and the air felt so oppressive she could scarcely breathe. Although the program had not yet begun, Diva wanted to turn around and go home.

The stage stood in the atrium of the mall, decorated like a cheap birthday cake. The throbbing house mix of children's music competed with the babble of human voices. It was like being inside a beehive.

"Diva darling!" A woman with an ID card dangling around her neck rushed to meet her. "Thank you so much for coming. The competition is about to start."

Diva smiled politely and sat in the chair that had been prepared for her.

A man wearing sunglasses appeared from nowhere and held out his hand: "Good afternoon. I'm Hari, the second member of the panel." "Diva, how do you do! I'm Tetty, from the Sunshine Foundation. The children are all from my modeling school. Oh, and I'm number three on today's panel of judges. Why, you look even more gorgeous in person!"

"I do, don't I?" Diva replied in a flat voice. Suddenly she decided that her work on the panel was more important than any task that even the president might undertake over the next few hours.

She looked at the children's faces. Their innocence was about to be ruined by their eagerness to be chosen as the most beautiful contestant on stage today. Diva was disturbed by the makeup smeared all over their faces. It was completely unnecessary. Makeup was for women who had begun to lose their beauty or, to be more precise, believed that they had begun to fade. They needed to make an extra effort to appear pretty. These children didn't.

Diva looked at the girls' tiny feet. They all wore boots. With high heels. Super-mini skirts. Tank tops. And jackets with animal skin motifs. Despite their youthfulness, the girls were covered in jewelry making them look like gang molls and whores.

Once the competition started, Diva ignored her pen and the judge's work sheets, divided into columns. She folded her hands, sat back in her chair, and stared carefully at each child. The members of the organizing committee began to whisper to each other suspiciously. Tetty and Hari glanced at each other, concerned that the chief judge was not writing anything at all. Diva knew what they were thinking, but she didn't care. None of them would understand how she felt.

The little girls sashayed to the front of the stage, turned and posed, wearing their most artificial smiles. From time to time one would glanced toward her parents, who were nervous, too, afraid that their child might forget the right number of steps to take or might not assume a particular pose in the way they had practiced together for the past month.

By the age of fifteen, many of them would be as tall as they ever would be. At seventeen, a number would be overweight. Today's winner would probably dump the whole catwalk routine and become a research scientist. The girl everyone considered the least attractive today might be a top model by the time she was twenty. There were so many possibilities and uncertainties in life that Diva could find no grounds on which to choose a winner. And what did winning mean, anyway? Humiliating another child and making her feel ugly? Forcing her parents to work themselves into the ground to make her feel better, before sending her off to other competitions, better equipped with more "potent" weapons? Better prepared? More artificial?

Today should have been like a party. The girls should have been able to laugh out loud. Dance. Twirl. Fall over. Throw off their clothes and run around naked. Play anything they wanted to play. No rules and no expectations.

Diva was deeply disturbed by what she was seeing.

One child, with tufts of hair sticking straight into the air like bell towers, walked toward the front of the stage as if she were a professional model. She glared at the panel, one member after another, trying to impress them. Her jacket, as bright as a Stabilo coloring pen, was draped with a wool shawl which the girl waved flirtatiously. As a finale, she suddenly arched her back like a snake and pursed her tiny lips coquettishly, as if to blow each judge a kiss.

Surprised, the audience roared with delight. The applause was tumultuous.

"Aren't kids amazing these days?" Hari whispered as he leaned toward Diva.

Diva swallowed hard. She was trying not to lose her lunch.

There were seventeen contestants, who might have been seventeen little laxatives given the way they made her stomach churn. Had there been any more, Diva could have emptied her stomach of a whole rice-barn.

It was time for the three judges to make their decision.

"Well, Hari, what did you think?" Tetty asked with exaggerated animation, conscious of the need to satisfy parents who paid outrageous fees for their babies to attend her children's club. "I really liked number eleven. Wasn't she wonderful? What about you, darling?"

"You'll see soon enough," Diva calmly replied.

Hari was busy adding up his scores. "I think we're in complete agreement, Tetty."

"Good!' said Diva, grabbing the tabulations out of his hand. "It's all decided. I'll make the announcement, if I may."

Standing at the front of the stage, Diva spoke into the microphone: "Good afternoon, girls, mothers and fathers. I have the names of the winners in both categories right here in my hands. Let's begin straight away, shall we?"

One by one, the winning contestants returned to the stage as their names were called, their faces shining. After applause died away for the last winner, Diva returned to the microphone. "Sweet young ladies, the girls you see here before you on the stage were chosen because they were the ones most capable of pretending that they were adults. We had to choose them because their moms and dads have paid their registration fees and bought them expensive clothes to wear. In fact, no one has won today, and no one has lost. Today, you are all very cute and pretty. One day, you might be short and fat and covered in pimples.

"Please remember to play real games when you get home. Don't bother about high heels. Or smearing yourself with makeup. Believe me, you'll find high heels and lipstick rather boring once you've grown up. Play as much as you can now. If you want to be beautiful, don't wait for someone else to tell you how you look. I'll give you a special spell to make you beautiful. This is how it works: Go to the mirror and repeat over and over, 'I'm beautiful, I'm beautiful, I'm beautiful.' And I guarantee you that you will be beautiful; always and forever. Amen. Do you understand what I'm saying?"

A sudden silence fell over the noisy atrium. The girls listened to Diva, their mouths agape. Mothers and fathers held hands, trying to gain strength from the physical contact. The clowns at the edge of the stage stopped their performance. The emcee was lost for words. The members of the organizing committee anxiously bowed their heads. Their whole program had been ruined.

Only one face remained unchanged. Absolutely indifferent to the tornado raging around her, with calm proud steps, Diva left the stage. And walked straight toward the exit.

"Straight home, Miss?" her chauffeur, Ahmad, asked.

"Straight home, please."

On the way, Diva gnawed at her bottom lip. It was something she always did when she was excited. She was thinking of the children and how they had listened to her. She hoped they had understood what she was trying to tell them. She hoped she had been able to change the way they thought. Hope.

Diva remembered her own body as a girl. She had been tall for her age and as thin as her little finger. Her body was rectangular when all the other girls had begun to develop curves. The other girls had luxurious heads of hair but her locks were straight and boring. Her thin face suggested that she never had enough to eat. Because her legs were so long and her feet so narrow, the donated shoes that came as presents to the orphanage never fit.

All the voices claimed that she was weird and ugly, all but one: her own. And look at her now. She owed nothing to other people praising her left and right and everything to her own belief that she was truly beautiful. Once she accepted that, everything else naturally followed. She didn't need to do a thing.

I hope they understand... She entered her house, still biting her lower lip.

The Republic of Indonesia Broadcasting Service. Vegetable prices: chilies were slowly climbing; onions were falling; potatoes had plunged; cabbages were flooding the market; eggplant was today's prima donna; ginger was walking a tightrope.

It was a veritable circus of commodities.

In the fields, everything grew at its own pace. The tomatoes never made a fuss if they were invaded by worms. They didn't panic if they were covered with insecticide. Death meant nothing to them because they knew they would live again. It was only the farmers who worked themselves half to death, simply so they could stay alive.

No one could remember the last time people planted vegetables for pleasure. To care for the beautiful green life while it worked its way through the various layers of soil. When people went to the market and were given fruit and vegetables at no cost. When farmers were proud of their produce, sold what they grew in order to earn enough to cover their expenses, then gave the rest away. When no one dared take more of these beauties than they could use, for fear that they would rot and be wasted.

The telephone rang. Diva turned down the radio.

"Yes, hello?"

"Hi, babe."

On hearing the voice of Nanda, a client, Diva frowned. "Have we arranged a time?" she asked him immediately.

"What about now?"

Diva turned her face away from the telephone and laughed. "You're turning into a big spender! Maybe I'm not charging you enough. Or are you suddenly addicted to me?"

Nanda laughed out loud. He enjoyed Diva's cruel sense of humor. Her honesty was like an oasis in the middle of a desert of intolerable politeness.

"Diva, to be honest, I just want to have dinner with you. Nothing more."

"You can have more if you have the money."

Again his laugh boomed from the other end of the telephone.

Diva checked the list of appointments on her cellphone. "You're in luck. I'm free tonight. Pick me up at eight, OK? Bye."

Remembering the eight-month-old orange sapling in her back garden, Diva picked up a spray can of liquid fertilizer and headed outside.

The man began to drool as soon as Diva walked through the door. He didn't know which excited him more: the tight black Lycra top that clung to her like a second skin or her eyes that cut through the air like samurai swords thirsting for blood.

"I'm hungry," she said spontaneously. "I could eat you alive."

Her words made it even more difficult for him to control himself. But no matter how he felt, Diva was a professional, just as he was. She made it quite clear that no one touched her, not even a quick welcoming hug, without first coming to a financial arrangement. Nanda didn't want to spoil the evening by getting to that point too quickly. Because once that happened, everything thereafter was very different.

He needed Diva for other things.

The restaurant had stopped accepting orders half an hour earlier. In fifteen minutes, it would close completely. A row of determined waiters hovered impatiently, staring at the two customers who showed no sign of leaving.

"You really said that in front of all the parents? You're crazy… crazy!" Nanda was laughing so boisterously, he could hardly speak.

"Isn't nice to be in your shoes, a lunatic who thinks that everybody else is crazy."

"All right, take it easy. I would never willingly take my kid to a mall anyway! I leave that to my wife. She likes to meet her parents there."

"I wasn't attacking you. It's no sin. I merely said that a mall on weekends is the perfect place to show off middle-class kids under the age of five, while preparing them for a lifetime of conspicuous consumption. That's the time when parents play Ken and Barbie, just the way their children do. Except they use their kids as dolls."

"And what's wrong with that?" Nanda asked, annoyed.

"Nothing. As long as the parents know what they're doing and are not pretending to be something they're not. I can't stand people who use their kids as an excuse to show the world that they've been good parents. They don't have a clue what they are doing. How can they train their children when they haven't learnt a thing themselves? The results are appalling. Or maybe playing Ken and Barbie is some sort of compensation for all the bother their kids inflict on them."

"You're incredibly cruel." Nanda clicked his tongue several times.

"And you're incredibly stupid," Diva replied calmly. "Answer me this. Which one of you decided to have children? Be honest."

"We both did. Although I have to admit that our parents couldn't wait to hold their grandchildren. 'Don't leave it too long,' they kept saying. 'If you don't start soon, you won't be able to have any. Don't put your career before your family. Children bring their own blessing.'"

Diva giggled. "Their own children still behave like kids but somehow it's time to start all over again."

"The cuter the kids are, the more their grandparents adore them. Except at potty time, then it's—'Ugh! Your kid just pooped its pants!'—and they hand them straight back."

"Enough! I'm exhausted." Diva gathered her things. "Sometimes I think I should be paying *you* to entertain *me*."

As they stood, the waiters let out a collective sigh of relief.

Soon, Nanda's expensive jeep was speeding down empty streets. There was no other sound other than the hum of the tires against the asphalt. No music. No conversation. The tires turned more slowly as the vehicle approached a hotel.

"Are you serious?" Diva asked, glancing at him from the corner of her eyes. "I really thought you only wanted to have dinner."

The jeep turned into the courtyard of the hotel and stopped. Nanda bowed his head.

"Don't torture yourself. You can't even have a little fun without worrying."

His expression became even more serious.

"Is this how you live your life? I told you how easy it is for most people to make fools of themselves. So don't make yourself miserable by putting on such a sad face."

Suddenly the man looked up. He was struggling with something. Diva was surprised to see a look in his eyes which she had never seen before.

"Diva, if I have to pay for a little fun I'd rather pay you for having dinner with me than... Oh, you know. It probably sounds stupid, but that is what I'd prefer to think I was paying for, even if..."

Diva slowly shook her head. "I'm not that stupid, Nanda, even if you are. And I have no intention of acting as though I am. Any truth that can be bought and sold isn't a truth at all. I have something to sell, as you do. We wouldn't survive, either of us, if we didn't recognize that. Don't ruin the only way you have to escape from the mess you've made of your life to get back to your true self. Just now I saw you struggling with yourself to be honest. You cursed Diva the Prostitute because she puts a price on what she has to offer you. Poor, poor Diva." The young woman bowed her head and played with a corner of her jacket.

Turning off the motor, Nanda resolved to get rid of the confusion inside his head. "All right, let's get out," he said, touching Diva's hand.

In the lonely hotel room, Nanda clung to Diva's relaxed body for as long as he had the right to do so. Their strenuous activity had made no impression on him. None at all. It was all like a bad dream. He felt as though he had raped his mother or his little sister. Just so that he could give her an envelope filled with cash.

Nanda buried his face deeper into the nape of Diva's neck.

He began to cry, very softly. There was no language through which he could express his feelings. The only language he knew spoke through numbers.

If only he could put a love letter in the envelope. Pour out his gratitude. Without writing a single word.

For someone like Diva, the days passed quickly. Even if sometimes she had to ignore her own feelings. As she did tonight.

"Hello, gorgeous," the gray-haired man whined as he took off his thick glasses. His name was Margono, a man who was now well past sixty and a professor of marketing at one of Indonesia's top universities.

"Hello to you," she replied gently. "How is our nation's leading intellectual today?"

The man laughed: "I like it when you mock me. Your favorite teacher has an overwhelming urge: for you!"

"In that case, you're lucky you teach in one of the more lucrative departments of the university. The real professors couldn't afford me at all. Or have you found some new educational project to take advantage of?"

"Education is a business these days, young lady, like anything else. The world runs on money and that applies to universities as well."

"As long as you don't have to live in your Ivory Tower, you're fine. Is that it?"

"Young lady, I may be old but I still prefer the best. And that includes you."

"Don't think you can flatter me so easily."

"Where is the thong I asked for? Are you wearing it?"

Diva nodded. "If you want me to parade for you, that will cost extra. Are you sure you can afford all this?"

The old man rubbed his hands together. He was burning with desire. In his excitement, he fumbled through his briefcase. Taking out a bottle, he swallowed two pills.

"They say these are as good as Viagra. Better, in fact. Viagra only works on the sexual organ. These stimulate the brain. One of my colleagues is going to a symposium in Boston soon. I'll ask him to bring me back a big bottle!"

Diva realized that she had come face to face with a dirty old man who was still trying to sharpen his horn even if it had begun to retreat inside his body. She wanted to grab the mirror and show him what he really looked like.

Professor Margono looked at his watch. "We have to wait ten minutes. They say that it takes ten minutes for the pills to be effective. Perhaps fifteen minutes, at most."

Diva sat down and folded her hands in her lap. "How far have you got with your new book on *Das Kapital,* Professor?"

"Not very far at all; the contributors are always fighting with each other. I find it all very confusing. One contributor wants to talk about historical materialism. Another is only interested in situational ethics. I've simply told them to write about whatever they want. When they're finished, I'll hire a chief editor to knock the volume into some sort of shape."

"I could do it for you," Diva offered enthusiastically. "But I wouldn't start with Marx, or finish with him either, for that matter. I've done a lot of reading already. Marx needs to be seen in the context of Hegel, Feuerbach, Kant and Fichte. The subsequent effects of his thought are important too, particularly on Gramsci and the neo-Gramscians. And don't forget Habermas. He has so many interesting things to say, especially about social emancipation. The most important thing about Marx is how he relates to our society today and how this relates to the origins of his thought, what he really believed."

Professor Margono cut her off with a superior laugh. "My sweet, I know that you are smarter than any of my lecturers but, really, what are you? I don't mean to offend you but..."

Diva shrugged.

"I mean you've never studied in a university. You don't have a higher degree. You're not a professor," Professor Margono stopped, then quickly corrected himself: "Though I'm sure you're quite capable of doing all those things."

"Isn't there a place for someone who simply enjoys ideas for their own sake?"

"You have to do these things the right way. Follow the proper curriculum, take the examinations, defend your thesis. We don't simply give degrees away."

"The problem is that I don't believe in your system, professor," she retorted. "It doesn't teach people to think properly, to see all sides of the issues, to take a balanced position. So when your so-called 'scholars' discuss a topic, they only confuse people. Their conclusions are never consistent. Whether it be in the fields of scholarship, religion, or culture, their arrogance is incredible, all because of the limited nature of their training. They will never look at the full context of anything."

"All right, I surrender! Stop, stop!" he pleaded desperately. "I'll sell you a diploma. I'll make you a lecturer. One of my friends can arrange the whole thing. We'll make you a doctor straight off."

"Don't bother," Diva casually replied. "One day I'll have my own school, a school that gives its students knowledge, not just degrees."

"Great! I'd like to teach there," he said, teasing her.

"You can't. All the students would be exactly like you, professor. Pity our poor people."

"Call me Margono, gorgeous."

Diva was speechless, realizing they had been talking on different wavelengths.

Nervously, Professor Margono began turning his watch around and around. "It's been eleven minutes and nothing has happened yet."

"Don't force yourself, professor." She smiled a wry smile. "I can go. You'll be entitled to a full refund."

"Why isn't it working?" He was overwhelmed with panic. "Maybe you have to take off all your clothes. Or do something! Hurry…"

Slowly, Diva began removing her garments, one by one.

"That's better."

Professor Margono blinked like a barn owl. He began to slobber. "Come here, you!" he shouted wildly. As Diva approached him, he swooped on her, intent on showing no mercy.

He tried and tried. Fifteen minutes passed… nineteen… twenty… twenty-two… eventually he gave up. He was tired. Exhausted from pursuing what he couldn't have.

"Perhaps you should wait until your friend brings you back a big bottle, professor," Diva said, as she stood up and started to gather her clothes.

Professor Margono drooped, just like his penis. Unable to say a single word.

Diva walked over to the envelope and took half the money from it.

"This is for the strip-tease," she said, as she left the room, "and to replace the thong you tore."

The door closed behind her.

8

"What a Small World!"

"Couldn't you just fall in love with her?" asked Ruben as he pressed the manuscript to his breast.

Dhimas snatched the pages back. "Thank heavens she's only a character in a story," he responded.

"You did it on purpose, didn't you? The Falling Star is a lot like me. I think she's a female version of me."

"In your dreams."

"Oh, please. How can you be jealous of a character in a story you're writing?"

"Jealous? I was rescuing her: from you! How can I let you compare yourself with her?"

"This is weird. Now we're fighting over a woman who doesn't even exist!" Ruben cackled.

"And we're both gay!"

"I think we should take a break."

"You're right."

At ease, they both lay back. Before long, however, Ruben was on his way to the kitchen, to make a cup of coffee.

"Aren't you afraid your heart will explode? How many cups of coffee have you had today?"

"We all have to die sooner or later," Ruben called out from the kitchen. "And I'll be proud of my Arabica-caffeinated corpse."

"No kidding. When you're dead, people will be able to use your grave to make themselves coffee. All they'll need to do is bring some hot water and a cup with them."

Ruben searched for something to nibble on while his coffee cooled. Dhimas stretched out and flicked through a magazine. They both came briefly back to earth.

"Don't you think it's a waste of time reading those gossip magazines?"

"Lighten up, Ruben. I'm interested in knowing what's happening in the world."

"Sure, sure. I'm the boring, serious one." Ruben sat next to him, reading the magazine over Dhimas' shoulder. "Is anything exciting happening in the world of celebrities?"

Dhimas flicked through the magazine again, then suddenly stopped. "As a matter of fact, yes, I think there is," he mumbled.

"Tell me. This nerdy boy is all ears."

"Look at this," Dhimas held out the article, illustrated with a large photograph of a man. "Do you still remember this guy?"

Ruben stared intently at the picture. "Ferré?"

"Yep, Ferré. He graduated from Berkeley. We met him at an Indonesian Student Association gathering in D.C. What year was that?"

"Oh, I remember him. We talked a little. Neither of us was interested in the event, so we immediately had something in common. He lived in America since junior high school, so why would he come to an Indonesian Student gathering?"

"One of the consulate gang, maybe?"

"Worse. One of the immigrant gang. I think he was only there to keep a friend company."

"Miranda's little brother, wasn't it? What was his name?"

"Rafael."

"That's right, Rafael! Miranda and I were neighbors in Kebayoran Baru when I was growing up. I used to play at her house a lot."

"What a small world!" Ruben exclaimed. "Rafael stayed in my flat when he first came to Baltimore. He only lasted two weeks, couldn't stand Baltimore. There wasn't anything to interest him, he said. So he headed back to San Francisco. And now his friend is a big-time celebrity! If this Ferré guy had stayed in America, he'd be a speck of dust in a vast desert. Or maybe he wouldn't exist at all."

"Don't be so harsh. He obviously has talent. And, God, he's good looking!"

"Not bad."

Dhimas read the article carefully. "Hey, do you know something?"

"What? Is he gay?"

"No, he's just like our Knight."

"Why am I not surprised?"

"Age twenty-nine. Single. A managing director already, in a multinational company! Perfect."

"But don't forget," Ruben said, waving a finger at him. "He might be an immigrant there, but coming back here, he's an 'import' here, a brown expatriate. No wonder he rose as quickly as he did."

"Will you stop being so cynical?"

9

No Strings Attached

Ferré had a picture in his mind: the two of them could see them together on a rare Sunday afternoon. As a mist of fine rain drew a curtain across the window, they sat on the carpet in his study, looking at a *manga* which Rana had given him: *Kariage Kun.*

"Do you still collect Japanese comics?"

"Of course! I love reading them," Rana replied proudly. "Don't you?"

"Sure."

"You're not reading it just because I gave it to you?"

"No, Princess."

They were silent for a long time.

"Rana, are you okay?"

Her eyes glistened, as she struggled to contain herself. "I melt each time you call me Princess," she said softly.

"Does your husband ever feel jealous of *Kariage*?" he continued, ignoring her reply.

"Sometimes. Especially when he doesn't know why I'm laughing."

"Really? I love watching you read *Kariage*."

Rana's eyes shone again. "Why?"

"I love to see you lost in your own world. So totally absorbed that you don't even know where you are. You wrinkle up your forehead. Then, suddenly, you start laughing, and only you know the reason why. It's cute."

"You really know how to love me, Ferré."

I love you with my whole heart, Princess. I don't know
if it's the right way or not. I don't care whether you see
me or not. I don't care whether you're happy because of
me or because of something inside of you.

"What's this?" Ferré asked as she offered him a pencil. It was an ugly wooden pencil, roughly sharpened by a penknife, which she had taken from a restaurant they had been to.

"Let's make a bet."

"What sort of bet, Princess?" Ferré asked meekly.

"Each time one of us misses the other one, we have to make a line on a piece of paper. We'll do it all day, from the moment we wake up until it's time to go to sleep. Then, the next time we see each other we bring our pieces of paper and see who has the most lines. But you have to be honest, all right? There'll be trouble if you don't."

After briefly considering the proposal, Ferré smiled. "What's the prize?"

"The one with the least number of lines has to write a poem."

"A poem? That's not fair. You're a writer, you can do it easily."

"You're wrong, dear. It takes more than journalistic skill to compose a poem. Do you remember when I asked you whether you made any room for inspiration in your work? The poet doesn't hear inspiration knocking at the door. Inspiration smashes down the walls of his house, without asking whether it can enter or not."

Inspiration. Again the word pushed Ferré down the long dark corridors of his childhood. One memory begot another.

Once I was a poet. The spirit of a dead poet possessed
my tiny body. Every word I spoke was a lustrous pearl.
But the pearls looked strange among the stones in the

*river. My thoughts were a million mazes trapped in a
tiny matchbox. I was a complete anomaly.*

"You haven't got a chance, dear. I'll win for sure. You'd better
start composing your poem right away," Rana whispered into his
ear.

Ferré smiled as he played with the pencil. "You know I can never
write a poem."

"So you'd better not lose." She took his hand and kissed it
softly.

Rain pattered on the window.

*I've won the bet, fair and square. Long before you gave
me pencil and paper. Because each drop of rain says: "I
miss you." We don't need paper, we don't need to draw
lines. Just hold my heart and listen to each beat.
That's how much I need you, Princess.*

"Ferré…"

"Yes?"

"I win."

"Already?"

"I miss you."

"Have you ever heard of telepathy?"

"Why?"

"Because I was thinking the same thing."

"I love you," Rana said as she held his hand more tightly.

"I love you too, Princess."

As the tedious meeting with his financial staff dragged on,
thoughts of Rana exploded in Ferré's head like firecrackers. And
it was all due to this, the wooden pencil Rana had given him. He
carried it in his pocket everywhere he went.

His left hand drew lines on a piece of paper, one line every two
minutes.

There is a reason it is called the living heart. It beats softly like the wind caressing the sky. It reaches out gently like the splashing foam. The air is love's true blood. Love's spirit lives in my breast.

Ferré's staff had begun to notice their boss's unusual behavior: his breathing had become deeper, gentler. Perhaps he was practicing his *tai chi* exercises.

Every Sunday he felt exactly the same: absolutely miserable. When he was in the office, he dreamed of Sunday. When Sunday arrived, his dreams had nowhere to go. And, unlike the office, there was nothing to distract him at home.

Across the road, the silver car had returned yet again, while he hadn't gone out all day. He could no longer escape into the *Kariage Kun* comic. It simply wasn't funny any more. Only one thing could help: the telephone. If someone rang him or if he could ring that someone. As long as it was the right someone: Rana. *Telepathy is nonsense,* he grumbled to himself. *Which is why God knew from all eternity that Alexander Graham Bell would one day have to invent the telephone.*

Ferré glanced out the front window again at the row of immaculately maintained luxury town houses, the residence of choice for successful young singles. Suddenly, he felt very lonely: He was a successful young loser.

Five minutes later Ferré realized the utter stupidity of his situation. He was famous for his efficient and effective use of time. Yet now he had wasted a whole half day doing nothing. A few weeks ago he still thought himself capable of concealing his situation and he had failed completely. He was having dinner with Rafael one night when his friend caught him red-handed. His cellphone had rung and interrupted their conversation.

Ferré turned his back on Rafael. "Hey, Rana? Has the piece been published? Sure! When can I see it?"

"Rana? The reporter?" Rafael asked, as soon as Ferré turned around.

"Yup."

"You really like her."

"Don't kid yourself."

"I can see it as plainly as I can see this spoon."

"You're crazy," Ferré replied defensively. "She's married."

"So? If you like her, you like her. It doesn't matter whether she's married or not."

Ferré laughed. "Rafael, we're not college boys any more. I'll be thirty in a few months. Sure there are lots of men in their fifties who can't keep their eyes off every sweet young thing who walks by, but I'm not like that."

Suddenly Ferré's phone rang again.

"Hello," he said uncertainly.

"Hi!" It was the same energetic voice, filled with vitality and innocent joy. This time, Ferré stood up and walked away from the table to continue the conversation.

Rafael smiled. Five minutes later, his friend returned.

"Rana again?"

"Yes," was the curt response.

"You really do like her."

"Stop it."

Their meals arrived.

"Ferré," Rafael said, pausing between bites, "the light isn't very good here, and it's even worse where you were standing, but your face is shining so brightly, you could dazzle us all."

"Give me a break!" Ferré said sharply, blushing.

We all carry the sun inside ourselves. Some of us show it, some don't. My sun shines non-stop, twenty-four

*hours a day. Do you have some washing you'd like to
dry? Do you have some rubbish you want to burn? Let
me shine my face in your direction.*

To Ferré, this continual excitement was some sort of progress.
To Rafael, it was total self-indulgence. And he had said so, in no
uncertain terms. For Ferré, there was nothing to be gained by
wasting his life in this way.

Ferré glanced at his watch anxiously.

*Come on, Princess, crack your whip. Make time run
more quickly. Make it mean something.*

Suddenly, he was struck by a disturbing thought. Perhaps this
was the way things really were: love doesn't set anyone free, that's a
utopian idea. Love is a tyrant. It ties you up in chains and throws
you into a dark dungeon.

Now he understood it all. His golden reputation, his platinum
career, meant nothing at a time like this. They crumbled to dust in
front of the palace of the greatest drug king of all: Love. Ferré felt
small, weak, completely drugged.

RANA

It was a matter of enormous regret to Rana that Arwin knew her
menstrual cycle so precisely. She had tried everything to keep him
at a distance, from going to bed early to pleading a headache. And
now she had run out of excuses.

Rana realized that the longer this situation continued, the more
desperate her husband would become: like a hungry lion, ready
to pounce at the first opportunity. Even worse, he might become
suspicious. They had agreed to have a child this year, which meant
that they needed to make extra effort if they were to be successful.

Her agony was intense.

Arwin emerged from the bathroom, ready for bed.

Rana looked at her husband and the expression on his face. It was one she knew well. Like a scalded cat, she drew even further onto her side of the bed.

"You're not taking the pill any more, are you?" he asked.

"Of course not," Rana swallowed her lie. *Every day. Microgynon is more important to me than lunch. I take it every day. I can't afford not to.*

He switched off the light.

Rana turned her back to him and yawned loudly several times, before closing her eyes firmly. Intently she listened to every sound. Each rustle of the sheets made her heart race.

She felt Arwin's arms embracing her from the back, his warm breath on her neck, his deliberate caresses.

"Rana," he whispered. "Your hands are as cold as ice. Why?"

"Are they really?" she asked in a trembling voice.

"Are you sure you're well?"

"Not entirely. I think I've got a touch of the flu." *Don't, please don't do that. I beg you.*

"Do you want me to make you feel better?" Arwin pleaded. With these words, his victory was usually assured. And he had to succeed tonight. He had waited too long.

Only the walls and ceiling heard Rana moan and saw the pain on her face. As she surrendered, her silent cry rang out: *Ferré, help me. I'm being raped.*

DHIMAS AND RUBEN

"How are our Knight and his Princess?" Ruben asked, placing one hand on Dhimas' shoulder.

Dhimas continued typing.

"Things are bad and getting worse."

"How bad?"

"Can you imagine what it must be like to be imprisoned in your own identity? When even your bed is a living hell?"

"Heaven sounds so utterly simple in contrast. The word 'Hello' on the telephone, or 'Hi!' across a crowded room."

Suddenly Dhimas stopped typing and spun around. He looked at Ruben. "Writing about these two people makes me realize how lucky I am," he said earnestly. "You make me feel proud of myself, Ruben. You give our relationship a purpose. We're best friends. We share our whole lives with each other."

"We're free. That's the key," Ruben replied gently. "We've never chained ourselves to each other. No strings attached. Love should liberate people, not bind them. Why should we seek to destroy it by enslaving each other?"

SUPERNOVA

The inbox clicked open. One e-mail after another popped into view.

>Supernova, a person I know has lost someone they
>cared about. I don't feel very sympathetic. It makes
>me sad to see them sorry when they should be glad.

I feel exactly the same way. For the same reason. But go to them anyway. Realize that they are crying because they are still lost in a dream. I feel the same way about weddings. Most couples have no idea what they're doing. And everyone is so happy. Our prayers are needed on both occasions: many prayers. Be there and pray for them.

>Supernova, I really enjoy your articles on pop culture
>and postmodernism. I've read them all and I think
>you're a post-structuralist. You're opposed to all
structures.
>Do you agree?

I am "post" everything you believed last year, yesterday,
and even a few moments ago. We are all evolving. You
can speed up the process by not categorizing everyone
and everything. Stop worrying.

<send>

>Supernova, I can't help myself. I hate my parents but
>I'm afraid of them too. I don't know what to do any
>more. I don't know what I believe. I don't know what
>I want to be. They've spent years raising me and all
>I've done is waste the oxygen I breathe. Maybe they've
>stuffed my head with something. Some shit or other.

>I'd rather just take drugs. They get angry because
>they don't understand how good drugs are and how
>much life sucks. I don't want them to put me in a drug
>rehabilitation unit. Can we meet, Supernova? I'd do
>anything to help you. I just want to be useful.

Supernova wants to disinfect your mind. The first
infection you must cure is your hatred and fear. Not
for your parents, but for yourself. The one thing you
weren't taught is who you really are, which is why you
hate life and are afraid of it. Drugs can give you a very
tiny glimpse of heaven but they'll destroy your brain
cells in the process. They take far more from you than
they'll ever give. They are a totally destructive solution

to your problem. You can renew your mind, but not by ruining it. Everything depends on what you think, on what you want to think. The only way you can help Supernova is by destroying your old patterns. Blow up your mind. Renew yourself by getting rid of everything that stops life flowing spontaneously through you.

Supernova is everywhere. You—I—we are each part of something that is much bigger than ourselves. Believe me. Your very existence is useful. You don't need to meet me.

<send>

>Supernova, you're a virus.

Of course. What took you so long?

<send>

>Supernova, I'm a real fan of your kindergarten. But
>you need to be careful. If people ever found out what
>you are doing, they'd try to stop you. The sort of things
>you're saying on this website are really dangerous.
>They don't agree with the constitution or with our state
>ideology. They don't agree with what most people in our
>society think.I'm scared. I don't want this kindergarten
>to be closed down.

Thank you, thank you very much for your concern. But I'm not opposed to anything. I simply offer an alternative perspective. You are all tied up in the most incredible knots and I want to help you to escape. It is up to you to decide what you want to do. I don't care whether what I say agrees or not with what you and everyone else call the constitution, morality, cultural norms, or the state ideology. Comparisons mean nothing to me. I'm interested in offering you analogies, ways of thinking about life and building a better world. Nothing more than that. Am I ruining you or helping you to feel better? Answer the question for yourself.

10

Only Change is Permanent

As eight o'clock approached, Ferré's stalled life began to unfreeze as he made his way to Rana's office, where he'd promised to pick her up. His eyes found her immediately, standing there, waiting for him. They fled to the refuge of his abode.

They had hardly spoken a word before Rana whispered to Ferré, "I can't stay all night, Ferré. You'll have to take me home before morning."

Ferré quickly nodded.

As soon as their hands touched, time swept them into its orbit. Forced to squeeze the maximum intensity out of their few hours together, the two beings ran, galloped, sped like wild horses. A night flooded in adrenalin. A hot night, crazy for love, while the prison door was briefly open. Freedom in a small space. Accursed be Jakarta whose citizens grow old out on the highways.

FERRÉ

There are times when words are futile. In the stillness of Ferré's bed, they stared at the window, allowing their emotions to drift.

Despite the darkness, the world was extremely beautiful. A heavy rain fell across the golf course. Ferré felt as though he were looking at a mirror.

The drops of rain are so large, the world so vast, that I feel like a dwarf. Even though the world is covered with a blanket of mist, the closer you come the higher my fire burns.
Millions of drops wash over me,
but I can never have enough of you.
Princess, you soften the barren earth. I open myself utterly to you.

"Rana… please don't go home."

She did not reply. But he understood everything her quivering body told him.

"Rana, please don't cry."

"You've asked for the only two things I can never give you."

"Please don't say 'never'. It hurts when you say that."

"But what can we do?"

Ferré loosened his hold of her. "That's for you to answer, Princess. Not me."

"You don't understand. It is impossible."

Ferré clenched his jaw. They were heading toward the same interminable discussion and he didn't want to go there again.

"I have so many obligations. I'm not simply married to my husband. I'm married to his family, to his whole social class. It's easy for you, you're free. There's no comparison."

Ferré turned her body around and looked at her. "I'm not making any comparisons. Comparisons won't get us anywhere. But I know you're strong enough to break away. To set yourself free."

"Break away from what? Morality? Social expectations? We can't escape these things. Please see that I'm trying to be realistic."

"Can't you see that you're only hurting yourself? What's wrong with what we're doing, Rana? Is it wrong for me to love you as much as I do? Don't my feelings count for anything?"

Once more, Rana found herself trapped in the same old dilemma. She was tired.

"Maybe you'd better take me home," she said wearily.

"Maybe I should."

Ferré got up.

Happiness and sorrow chased each other around and around, like terrible specters. Ferré and Rana were two sparks of light, caught in the middle of the game and unable to move. While Time… Time was an old man who watched them in silence, holding his pendulum arrogantly in one hand, unable to stop its slow progress forward.

DHIMAS AND RUBEN

Dhimas' back was stiff and sore. He rose from his chair, took out his back roller, and stretched it up and down his spine.

Ruben watched his partner in silence.

"What are you looking at?"

"Do you know what Einstein said about time?"

"What? Time's back hurts?"

"Sort of. It stretches and contracts."

"I beg your pardon?"

"Time isn't constrained by the metal marks of the clock. What do the minutes mean? The hours? What is a day? Simply a way of distinguishing the light from the dark."

"Don't be such a pseudo-deconstructionist. Can you imagine what would happen to the world without minutes and hours?"

"Nothing. They are only units of measurement. They're not time itself. So, again I ask, what is time?"

"You tell me. Why should I have to answer all your questions?"

"It was a rhetorical question, you dunce."

"Whatever."

"Twenty-four hours, three hundred and sixty-five days, makes one year," Ruben started to explain. "A unit in a particular calendar system, which is only one of many in the world. Once you get to know time a little better, to see beyond its mechanical aspects, you can start to recognize its more individual characteristics. Einstein said time is elastic, like rubber. For example, when we visit your parents, a moment feels like an eon to me. But in the Barnes & Noble bookshop, I feel like I should pay someone to stop the Earth from moving on its axis."

"Apart from insulting my parents, what is the point you're trying to make?"

"OK, OK," said Ruben, excitedly rubbing his hands together. "There are three perspectives we can take on time. The first is mechanical, tick-tock, tick-tock, like the clock on the wall. The second is relative."

"Time at my parent's house compared to time in Barnes & Noble," Dhimas interrupted, still irked by Ruben's remark.

"Very clever. And the third type of time is illusory. It begins from the premise that, in fact, time does not exist."

"And what does that have to with my back roller?"

"The springs in your roller can expand and contract. On this third perspective, those springs don't even exist."

"So yesterday was an illusion, as was last year, and today."

"Listen, our brains are bipolar generators. Each time the mind receives some particular input, it sends that information in two different directions. One path leads to the cortex, where a limited number of attractors translate the stimulus—simplifying the smell, the feeling, whatever it is—so that it can fit into a category we recognize. In other words, the cortex organizes the chaos we continually experience in our daily lives. The other path, that one leading to the brainstem, provides more random processing. This is the chance generator, which turns the input into something that is unstructured or non-specific—or renders it so complicated it can no longer be translated into anything else at all. Matti Bergstrom, the Finnish scientist who first studied this subject, said that we are most conscious of the random side of the generator when we wake up. Until the cortex starts flooding us with information, our minds are empty and we can't remember a thing: what our name is, what we've done with our lives, how much money we have, who our partner is."

"I know that feeling well," Dhimas remarked. "It doesn't last very long. A few seconds, maybe."

"Time is a concept produced by the cortex translating the data it receives. The subconscious provides this particular service free of charge, as a means of compensation for our inability to understand the true nature of chaos."

"And what is the true nature of chaos?"

"Permanence. Eternity rests on chaos, Dhimas. And the cortex translates into the past, the present and the future."

"But why?"

"Why?" Ruben laughed out loud. "So that we can understand what it means to grow, to develop, to evolve. Life and death are only gateways to further experience. We choose to experience them both at the very moment we become embryos. The important thing is neither birth nor death, but what happens in between. Throughout life, we follow various rhythms. As our physical bodies mature, the cells in our body are continually replaced by new cells. Every sentient being experiences this same process. Time is a way of marking these natural changes."

"But isn't time an intellectual construct, completely separate from our bodies? The cells don't know anything about time, but they still keep on reproducing themselves without a care for the minutes and seconds that are passing. It's people like you and me who turn time into a straight line and agree to be bound by it."

"That's exactly it! Time comes from the fundamental human desire to control life and our own individual lives. The past, the present and the future are all part of the one moment in time: eternity."

"Well, if the future is an illusion, what about prophecy, clairvoyance, horoscopes and those sorts of things?"

"Nothing stands outside eternity. It is an unlimited matrix, filled with all sorts of possibilities and potentialities. Basically, all predictions speak about what might happen. When we decide that something will happen, we begin to make it happen. Whether these tendencies do actually become manifest or not doesn't matter in the end. There is no difference between what happens and what doesn't happen. That is what is so amazing about eternity!"

"So what you're saying is that we should understand reality from two different standpoints. One is local and relates to the brain as an empirical organ. The other is non-local and has to do with the presence of Pure Consciousness in every empirical experience, including the experience of the brain itself."

"Tsk, tsk, what a brilliant analysis. I'm truly impressed."

"Then what about the past? You can still see the traces of what we did yesterday, can't you?"

Ruben shrugged. "If you're so attached to your trash bin, sure."

"I'm serious. That is what has always bugged me about quantum theory. Take the moon, for example." Dhimas pointed outside the window. "The moon only becomes a quantum object when there is an observer to study it. Is that right?"

"It is."

"Then, logically, if the observer turns around, the moon should vanish. But everyone knows that the moon doesn't suddenly vanish when I go to bed or faint or something."

"Well, like our brains, our bodies and everything that exists also have two aspects. They have certain non-local elements, which make them quantum objects. And, on the other hand, they are also objects in the way classical physics understands objects. They possess a certain mass and their quantum waves are dispersed at such an extraordinarily slow rate that we seem to see their center as surrounded by an aura of continuity. We refer to this continuity as a 'consensus'. The moon stays in the sky even when I turn my back on it. Macro-objects are so complex that it takes a long time before we can translate the terms in which they have changed. This continuity is the basis of all memory."

"Are you saying that memory is only a residue?"

"More or less. Let me take this further. The brain produces about 14,000 thoughts a day, five million thoughts a year and 350 million over a lifetime," Ruben continued. "If most of those thoughts weren't repetitions of things we've thought before, or so utterly trivial that we didn't even notice them, we'd go crazy. From the point of view of quantum physics, nature is nothing more than a quantum soup which bombards our senses with millions of pieces of data every single second. We would be overwhelmed by chaos if we couldn't organize this data into manageable amounts. That's the function of the brain. The brain responds in seven different ways in order to maintain our sanity and is still able to present us with the entire universe the whole time."

"Seven different ways?"

Ruben sighed. "Get ready. This is going to take a bit."

"I'd be really grateful if you could keep it short."

"First, there is our response to life and death: the most fundamental response. Even lice have it. This response teaches us to see life as a jungle, a place of constant conflict, where our one goal is survival. Second, there is our self-awareness, the response we use to create our own identity. Beyond the first response, there is a need to reflect back on who we are. This is the point at which we come in contact with power, order, reward and punishment.

"Third is the relaxation response. The mind is so active in the constant confusion of the material world that, from time to time, it needs to rest. It needs to experience peace and quiet, and to know that there is something beyond the external world. When a person turns his gaze inward, the intuitive response, the fourth response, kicks in. The brain constantly seeks information from within and beyond the body. When the source of information is external, we call that objective knowledge. When it comes from within, it is intuitive. From the fourth stage on, our responses basically depend on what is deepest within ourselves.

"The fifth response is the creative response. It allows us to explore facts and to create new things. This ability is given to us at those mysterious moments when we are filled with what we sometimes call inspiration. Sixth is the visionary response. Our mind has the ability to make direct contact with the Pure Consciousness, which exists utterly beyond the material realm. It is at this level that magic occurs, those acts we call miracles.

"Seventh, the response beyond all responses. Our brains begin with a single cell, which has no mental functions at all. That cell comes from a spark of life. It belongs to no category. Even though billions of nerves depend on the brain, the brain is still rooted in the Pure Consciousness that is its ultimate source. At this level, thought becomes completely unnecessary.

"Through these seven different responses, the whole world is spread out before us. Everything depends on which response a person chooses to make. The brain has been prepared as a means for us to play with life. What we play, how we play, is up to each one of us."

"Now I understand what the sages mean when they say that the past and the future are only distractions, which lead us off into abstract mental illusions. Nothing is more important than this very moment."

"Yes. This is the moment when everything is present. Only at this moment can we feel the past and imagine the present. At this very moment, we are new and without limits. But as soon as we are caught up into the linearity of history, we are suspended within the most stupid understanding of life we can possibly have."

"So why do we regret the past and worry about the future?"

"Exactly!"

"But what if in ten years you've become an ugly, bald-headed professor, senile and absent-minded?"

"Don't even think of it."

"Sorry."

"I have a question for you, Dhimas. If life and death are part of our human experience, how can we ever escape them?"

"In the Presence of the Divine Being Who Is Never Born and Never Dies."

Ruben gave a broad smile. "That is the most beautiful sentence I've heard all day."

11

The Nature Lover

As a punishment for her outrageous behavior at the children's fashion competition, Diva was banned from the catwalk for a whole month. She felt as though she had been handed a treat because she now had more time to spend in her tiny garden. Financially, nothing changed. The alarm on her phone kept ringing and dollars kept flowing into her bank account.

Diva's routine did not change. After morning yoga, she exercised on the treadmill, drank two glasses of fruit juice and did stretching exercises. Under the shower, she carefully rubbed oils into her skin, washed her hair twice, followed by a vitamin conditioner. Then she applied a good moisturizer all over her body.

She knew that her work required her to be extremely fit and to look her absolute best. But she looked after her body for a more fundamental reason. She liked to think of it as the vehicle through which she faced life and she knew that each body is an astonishingly intricate work.

Tonight Diva was ready before her alarm rang. This, in itself, was extremely unusual.

This man was not a client. He was more like a friend. In fact, he was the only man whom Diva allowed to kiss her on the lips. The only man she had allowed to come into her living room, although no further than that. Diva refused to turn her house into a marketplace, where goods were bought and sold. Even though she knew she would never ask money of this man.

Soon a car entered her driveway. Diva leaped from her chair and rushed outside.

"Gio! *Como vai, querido?*"

"*Esto tudo bem, meu amor.*"

They kissed fondly.

"You're more beautiful than ever," Gio said as he caressed her hair. "You must be happy."

"When am I ever not happy?"

"Of course. You are the Sun I have always known. *Minha sol bonita.*" Gio kissed her gently on the forehead.

Gio was of Portuguese-Chinese descent and blessed with uniquely handsome features. He had moved from Jakarta to Rio de Janeiro a long time ago and had just finished a climbing expedition in the Andes. His skin still glowed.

"Would you like to have dinner first? To be honest, I find you far more appealing than anything they might serve up in a restaurant."

"From you, Diva, that is high praise indeed."

"Perhaps it is because we only meet once a year. If you still lived in Jakarta, I would probably be quite content with a TV dinner."

Gio laughed. "I don't believe you. You couldn't have changed that much."

"*Entao,*" Diva put her arms around his waist and pressed him against the wall. "So, what do you want? Dinner... or me?"

"Why not both?"

They kissed again. A longer, deeper kiss. Diva enjoyed every moment of this unusual experience. It was what she had most hoped for from this evening together.

"*Minha sol.* I could make love to you *esta hora,*" Gio whispered. "Here, now, this very moment."

"No, not here," she whispered back to him. "Let's go." She took his hand. "We'll use my car and driver. That way, we won't have to concentrate on the driving."

Gio laughed and gazed lovingly at his Sun.

DHIMAS AND RUBEN

"I can't stand it any longer!"

On hearing Dhimas' scream, Ruben rushed into the study. "What's wrong?" he asked in a panic. "Has the computer died? Did you forget to save something?"

"Read this," said Dhimas as he offered what he had just written to Ruben. The newly printed pages were still warm.

Ruben skimmed through them. "You've decided to improvise a bit, have you?"

"I knew you wouldn't like it."

"That's not true. I don't mind a few romantic sub-plots to spice up the story, as long as they're relevant to what we want to say."

"Oh, they are," Dhimas quickly replied. "They most definitely are. Please read the chapter more carefully."

Ruben read more slowly. "It seems that you're trying to suggest another side to the Falling Star. She is not completely bitter. There is still an emotional side to her character, passion, that sort of thing, blah blah blah. So what?"

"This new character, the... the Nature Lover! I want to keep writing about him. But he isn't really necessary, is he?"

Dhimas was so shy that Ruben was taken by surprise. He didn't know whether to be amused or angry. "Regretfully, I would have to say that he isn't."

"But I don't want to get rid of him."

"A few hours ago we were talking about whether love can transcend time and space, weren't we? I don't think we should get caught up in this excessive display of emotion."

"Please! Just a little bit! The story is that he has come back from doing some heroic thing and wants to propose to the Falling Star one last time, his only true love."

"It's a waste of good paper!"

"You are so unromantic!"

"Romance is only a metaphor, a way of hiding some more important truth."

"Never. Romance is a major part of love."

"What sort of love?"

"Have you never thought of God as the greatest lover of all?"

"God? What an example. He is the greatest everything," Ruben protested. "So yes, I suppose He is the most romantic being in the whole universe."

12

Un Sol Em Noite

Since meeting Diva, Gio had changed his perspective on the night. If Diva was the sun who scorched the earth during the day, the darkness of the night wasn't caused by her absence. The night sky was black because the sun had burned it, turning it to ash.

As if she could read his thoughts, Diva looked up from where she lay, snuggled against his chest. "I can tell this is going to be a beautiful night." Her voice was soft and filled with sincerity.

Gio caught his breath. "Do you remember our first night together?"

"Gracious! You make it sound like our wedding night." She stretched and took a deep breath.

"Well, maybe it was for me."

"Do you still have the room key you stole?"

"*Claro, querida.* I know it might sound silly to you, but I don't care."

Diva said nothing. She tried to think back to that particular night.

Diva no longer remembered many things, but Gio was lucky: their first night together lingered in her mind.

Gio had seemed no more than a boy, even though they were the same age. There was in his expression an innocence which he made no attempt to conceal. She had no idea where Gio had heard about her, although she could easily guess. Obviously it was enough to make him take empty his savings account.

At first Diva had thought that he was a wild upper-class kid, who was looking to add her to his portfolio so he could boast to his friends.

"This is all the money I have, every cent of it," he had said nervously. "I hope it won't be a disappointment."

Diva laughed. "The moment I saw you, I decided that you were my handsomest client ever. Now I think you're my funniest. Wouldn't you be better off buying books with that money? Or travelling? Or buying a ring for your girlfriend?"

Gio's voice was so soft she hardly heard him. "I've never had a girlfriend."

"You haven't?" She was amazed. "A good-looking guy like you has never had a girl-friend?"

"I mean nothing serious. Not really anyone at all, in fact."

"Why not?" She crossed her legs and sat back in the lounge chair.

"I've never really considered it. I'm always too busy."

"Working?"

"Exploring. Mountain climbing. Rafting. I usually go hiking during my free time."

"An adventurer," she whispered, sitting up. "Where have you been?"

The expression in Gio's eyes changed. She had touched on something that mattered a great deal to him. Enthusiastically he told her of his many expeditions: the mountains he had climbed, the rivers he had followed to their sources, first in Indonesia, then the Yuat, Watut and Waghi rivers in Papua New Guinea. After that, he had seldom returned home. The world was too vast for him to stay put in one place. He hiked through the Tiger Leap Gorge in China and along the Rekiak Glacier in Tibet. These experiences had shown him his true vocation. He was destined to conquer rivers, to conquer mountains, to go where few had been before. Eventually he landed a job with Sobek Mountain Travel, an international adventure tour company.

Diva listened to him in amazement. "I'd love to live like you do, climbing mountains, rafting," she murmured, lost in thought. Perched on Gio's boots, Diva had been transported from their room, to tread on every rock and pebble in the amazing places he had mentioned.

"Maybe, but I don't think you could. Your feet are as narrow as carrots."

Diva burst out laughing. People said all sorts of things about her feet every day, but she had never heard them compared to carrots. "I like you, Gio. I always like meeting people who are full of life."

"You seem so full of life," he replied candidly. "You remind me of the Tatshenshini River."

"In Alaska?" she asked, even more surprised. "Have you been there?"

"I was there two weeks ago," he replied simply. "It was summer, the late afternoon sky was like crystal. I reached the top of the gorge and stood there, looking down on the river far below me. The Tatshenshini cut its way across a steep mountain valley covered with tight rows of pine trees. I've never seen so many pine trees so close together. The nebulae in the sky were light green and they kept changing as the sun set, until the heavens were bright orange. The sky burned like a fire. And the river below me…" Gio shook his head in awe, as if he were still standing above the gorge, "was gold. It gleamed. And here and there, little specks of white froth leaped high into the air. Can you imagine what it looked like? So tranquil, and yet so wild, just like you."

Diva was carried along by his words. She was fascinated but also restless. There was still work to do. She began to bite her lower lip. "Thank you for making this simple transaction more pleasant."

It seemed unlikely that he was really as innocent as he appeared. Yet the expression on his face surpassed all words, and, for the second time that night, she was deeply moved by his simple appearance. "Are you all right?" she asked softly as she held his trembling body. He was covered in a fine cold sweat. Gio could scarcely move.

How could he express it: that Diva, with her long hair and naked body, was the most beautiful sight he had ever seen; that tonight felt like magic; every cell in his body was ready to blossom like a flower in spring; that his senses were filled with the most exquisite feelings he had ever known; that he was ready to become a man; that Diva was like the sun, the midnight sun, setting over the Tatshenshini River. She was *un sol em noite*, the sun shining in the darkness of the night.

The sun rose and fetched him a glass of water.

"Here, drink this." She seemed concerned about him.

After a long silence, Gio finally spoke. "I'm all right. It's just that… this is my first time."

Diva was startled. That explained everything.

Without thinking, she gently tightened her arms around his body and drew him into the warm blankets on the bed, holding him there for a long time. "Your first time shouldn't be like this, not with someone like me."

"I'm sure I won't regret this," Gio replied softly. "Not now. Not later." *You don't understand. I've just met a goddess.*

And Diva was horrified, horrified by the intensity in his voice, by the realization of how seldom she was ever exposed to people who were truly fully alive. Automatically, she began to bite her lip.

At once, Gio reached out to stop her. *"Nao fazer isto.* Don't," he whispered.

Slowly and deliberately, he touched her chin, separated her lips, and kissed her. Gio was no longer the nervous boy he had been a few hours ago. His metamorphosis was perfect.

Diva had never allowed anyone to kiss her lips before. But tonight she decided to allow him to do so. To allow herself to enjoy this rare experience. To feel the electricity that flowed from millions of tiny nerve ends when their lips met.

Diva enjoyed every moment of their night together. Although she did not touch his money, they both took something precious back from the hotel. Diva had the memory of her first kiss. Gio took the room key.

"Diva," Gio's voice drew her back from the undertow of her memory.

"Are you still the 'Five-Thousand-Dollar Girl'?"

Diva laughed, thinking of the falling exchange rate of the rupiah against the dollar amid the economic crisis. "At today's rate of exchange, it's more like the 'Fifteen-Hundred-Dollar Girl'! A dollar goes a lot farther these days. How else do you think I could afford to buy a new Mercedes? Complete with driver!"

Gio did not comment, but he shivered nervously.

"Don't worry. I'm not bound to anyone. I don't rely on anyone. No one keeps me and I don't keep anyone else. I'm not part of a larger operation. I'm purely and simply in business for myself."

"Come with me, Diva," Gio pulled her closer. "You know I'll never interfere with your freedom. Nothing will change."

Diva kissed Gio's arm. "And you know what my answer must be."

He closed his eyes in anger. "I love you," he whispered urgently. "I always have, no matter what you've wanted."

Diva turned toward him for a moment. "I've never wanted anything. Each moment is what it is. We can't hold on to events and take them with us into the future merely because we think they are beautiful. The only way to maintain their purity is to let them go. There is no other choice. You have so much life in you, Gio. So you know that to plan the future is to destroy it. Let other people spoil the past, by spending the rest of their days patching their fading memories, turning them into useless, rotting rags that they will wear forever. Believe me, Gio, you wouldn't want to live like that."

"Why must you always be such a pessimist?"

"I'm not a pessimist. There's a vast difference between pessimism and honesty. I'm telling you the truth, nothing more, and nothing less."

Gio understood what she was saying but he was reluctant to let go of her.

"We were not created to be bound to anyone or anything else. Never be afraid of freedom. Don't ever try to manipulate freedom. Make every moment new and special."

"*Minha sol,*" Gio moved his face slowly toward hers. "Let me be one with you. As fully as I can."

"*Meu vem,* my sky," Diva whispered. "The sun burns the night and the day, without distinguishing between the two. All it knows is existence: nothing else is. We will never be apart from each other, not for a single moment."

13

God is So Unromantic

By coincidence, they were both in Bandung. And by design, Rana had to struggle with her program, to see where she could fit Ferré in and for how long.

Her cellphone rang.

"Yes?'

"Well?

Rana didn't like it. It was as though they were dealing drugs. "Maybe. In an hour, OK?"

"An hour? But I'm already on my way."

"I'll try to be ready in half an hour. Three quarters of an hour at the most. Will that be all right?"

"I only have until six o'clock," Ferré reminded her, leaving Rana no room to maneuver.

"I'll try," she said in a flat voice. Given the chance, she would have said instead, "This isn't fair." She felt as if she were an acrobat on a high wire in a circus, juggling her life so that she could fit into Ferré's timetable. His agenda was on steroids and he found it hard to compromise. *Maybe we shouldn't bother meeting at all.*

"I'll see you, Princess."

"Ferré…"

"Yes?"

"Don't come in. Arwin's friends hang out there. Meet me out back, in the parking lot."

"Oh," Ferré replied, reluctantly. *Maybe we shouldn't bother meeting at all.*

Violent currents roiled beneath the tranquil surface. It was as if they were doing something wrong. Why did they always have to be in such a hurry? Why couldn't they relax and not meet now and then? Why were they behaving like traders on the exchange floor? Would it always be like this?

FERRÉ

The tensions vanished as soon as they were together. Playing hide-and-seek was exhausting, but somehow it paid off.

Three precious hours.

"My interview doesn't start until seven," said Rana, caressing Ferré's hair.

"Sure. But I still have to be at my dinner meeting."

"If we were married, you'd never be home, would you?"

"Probably not. But at least we wouldn't have to scheme to be together. We wouldn't always be looking around all the time: front and back, left and right."

Rana bowed her head for a moment. She felt guilty.

A phone rang. It was Rana's. They were both startled.

"Oops, I forgot to turn my phone off." Rana struggled out of bed.

"You don't have to answer it."

As soon as the name of the caller appeared, they looked at each other.

"Sorry," Rana said. Her voice was barely audible.

Ferré nodded. He struggled not to show his feelings.

Rana rushed off to the bathroom. Her low voice echoed through the closed door.

Ferré sighed. *I can still hear you, Princess. Why I am I stuck in this back-to-nature hotel room, without even a television?*

He looked around, desperate to find something, anything that would make a noise and cover the conversation coming from the bathroom. There was nothing. Zilch.

The sound of Rana's laughter, of Rana making suggestions, of Rana listening to Arwin talking. Ferré would have given anything, all that he owned, for a pair of ear plugs. Plugs that could shut out every sound, from the human voice to infrasonic and ultrasonic sounds, right through to the sound of his own inner voice.

*Princess, I wish I were deaf. Two samurai swords
made of words attack me, hacking my self-respect into
mincemeat. They mock me because I cannot answer
them back. They curse me, because I know I'm nothing.*

After a long time, the bathroom door finally opened. Any longer and Ferré would have cut his ears off.

Although Ferré tried to appear cold and indifferent, Rana knew she needed to make amends for her sin. They promised to meet again that night. Rana lied to her colleagues: suddenly she had a cousin in Bandung whom she simply had to visit, this and that. For the sake of being together, to meet her beloved when he came home from work, to watch him brush his teeth before bed.

"You're cute when you brush your teeth."
Ferré laughed, spurting a burst of white foam from his mouth.

"What?" he babbled, still laughing. "That is the most original thing anyone has ever said to me. I could search the whole world over and I'd never find anyone like you."

Rana laughed. "What are you talking about? I can't understand a word you're saying. But even more…." Her cellphone rang again. "I'll be back in a moment. That must be Gita," she said as she scampered out of the bathroom.

Ferré laughed, continuing to scatter foam into the basin.

"Oh no," he heard Rana moan. "Hello? Yes, I was on my way out to have dinner with the girls. You're not back already, are you?" Rana walked to a far corner of the bedroom.

Ferré's laughter vanished. Deliberately, he closed the bathroom door. Twice in the one night. It was as though he were being systematically poisoned.

Turning on the tap, he rinsed his mouth, gargling as hard as he could. *I don't want to hear a word.* He cleaned the spots of toothpaste he had sprayed onto the mirror and around the basin. Suddenly he felt very stupid. *Princess, my brain is ready to explode.*

He flushed the toilet, turned on the shower. The bathroom was filled with the sound of running water. But still he couldn't drown the sound of the voice in his head.

DHIMAS AND RUBEN

Ruben refused to give in. "If God is the greatest everything, then He must also be the most unromantic being in the universe."

"OK, OK," Dhimas interjected. "It was only an expression."

"I absolutely agree," Ruben replied, raising one thumb victoriously. "I've always felt that love has been badly promoted. One item with so many different meanings. What a waste! No wonder people have so many wrong ideas about what it is."

Dhimas thought of some of the different possibilities. "The love of mature adults for each other. The love of parents for their children. A citizen's love for his country...."

"Eros, philia, agape."

"If there are so many concepts, then maybe the word doesn't mean anything."

"Hold on!" Ruben said, sitting straight up. "Let's not jump to conclusions before we've examined all the data."

"All what data?" Dhimas moaned. He had thought they were making light afternoon conversation.

"We need to talk about the nature of love, not its various forms. Love between mature adults, between friends, toward a cat, a mouse, are all different forms of love. Think how many forms we need to examine before we can say anything definitive. Because the reality is that there are endless ways of showing love."

"Love makes people hate each other."

"Love makes people kill each other."

"People go to war for the sake of love."

"It's crazy! What is love?"

"I think love is a sort of pure energy. But when it is polluted, it turns into hatred. And those other categories we were talking about, contain various levels of pollution as well, some more, some less. The pollution comes from the mind. And when the mind is purified, all that remains is…"

Dhimas was startled: "…a desire to experience."

Love is a desire to experience? Ruben was amazed.

"To love is to experience," Dhimas repeated firmly. "It is the essence of everything. It is why we live, why we are prepared to die, why people have romances, have children, grandchildren, why they do what they do. Why they experience what they experience. The desire for experience is our most fundamental drive."

For a moment, neither man could speak. They were caught up in a moment beyond words.

Then, slowly, Dhimas spoke: "Something great and substantial wanted to reveal itself through experience. So it created the world. It manifests itself through human experience. Through us, Ruben."

"The strange attractor. Feedback is the result of the strange attractor turning back on itself. Questioning itself."

"Asking itself the only question that really matters."

14

As Big as Love Itself

Today was Rana's birthday. Her husband was overseeing the building of a mosque in Surabaya and could not be home. Ferré should have been happy but he wasn't. On the contrary, he was utterly confused. He couldn't concentrate on anything.

Rana had planned a small party at her house that night and invited him to come. The idea was ridiculous. He had refused, as politely as he could.

"Ferré, it's only a party," Rana pleaded. "There'll be lots of people. Why shouldn't you come too?"

"No reason why not, Princess. But I still can't."

"But I want people to see that we're friends. People know that we are, anyway. There's nothing to be paranoid about."

"I'm not being paranoid."

"If you feel uncomfortable coming on your own, bring Rafael."

"That's not the problem." Ferré found himself stifling a laugh. If Rafael knew that he was even considering going to Rana's house, Rafael would tie him to a lamp post.

"You've never seen my home, never even taken me home. I know where you live and what your place is like. Don't you want to know about mine?"

"It isn't the same, Princess."

"What is so difficult?

"You are so naïve sometimes."

"Please come?"

Ferré did not reply.

"Pleeeeease!"

"I'll try. I can't promise anything, but I will try."

A car was parked in the street, half off the road, half on. It had not moved for half an hour.

Inside the car, Ferré sat staring at the fences.

He was sure that Rana would be annoyed if she knew that he couldn't come to the party... *because...* Ferré pressed his head against the steering wheel. *Because he was jealous.* A strange sort of jealousy only he could understand.

From time to time, he raised his head and glanced down the street. Lots of cars had started arriving. Her house was right there. She was so close. The woman, not the simulacrum he knew in a dream. He could be with her in twenty or thirty steps at the most. But Ferré couldn't move an inch.

> *I can't move my feet toward you. I can't lift my face to*
> *see you. I would be haunted by millions of images of you*
> *with him. The two of you eating together, or making love*
> *on the dining table. You shouldn't be there at all. And*
> *I'm sorry, I'm not in the mood to be tortured like that.*

Ferré started his car and drove away.

> *I want to own you completely. The desire is like a single*
> *cell that grows and becomes a thousand cells. I want*
> *to keep the healthy cells, Princess, may they divide and*
> *multiply and live within our love. They formed all*
> *around us the moment we fell in love,*
> *and we never even knew.*

He could only hope that one day Rana might understand.

ARWIN

The walls of the café were brightly decorated with vivid paintings. But they faded in the aura projected by Arwin's own inner gloom.

His friend knew how Arwin was feeling, and tried to be circumspect, but there was no way. "I don't want to jump to any false conclusions but I have seen them together on more than one occasion. It might be worthwhile checking up on what your wife has been doing."

It explained a lot of things: why Rana had been so quiet, so cold and so distant; why she always seemed so disorganized; why she avoided family gatherings; why she seemed so lost in her own thoughts and was so sad and so glum; and especially why she cried to herself, a soft, gentle weeping, which sliced through him like a bamboo knife, particularly after they had finished making love.

"I know the man. His name is Ferré. My cousin studied with him at Berkeley."

Arwin gave a heavy sigh. "Rana told me she was writing an article about him." He tried to sound natural.

"The article appeared months ago. I saw them together two or three days ago. On Monday last week, I saw them at the Shangri-La Hotel. And Desi said she saw Rana in Bandung, having dinner at Chedi's with a man who looked just like Ferré."

"I'm sure they're just good friends," Arwin replied. His face was rigid. "You know what Rana is like. She wouldn't do that sort of thing."

Arwin's friend was completely unconvinced but he didn't want to antagonize Arwin any more than he already had. He nodded: "You're right. I'm sure they are just good friends. Forgive me for being suspicious. I didn't mean to hurt you. I was only concerned for your sake."

Arwin felt as though he wanted to make a mad dash to the top of the tallest building he could find and jump off.

DHIMAS AND RUBEN

The two men stared intently at the monitor, as if they were watching an adventure movie that was building up to the final battle scene.

"Do you really have to let him find out?" Ruben said anxiously.

"I had to. Otherwise nobody would change. He has his lesson to learn, too. But what do you think he'll do? Poor man. He really does love his wife."

"Well, strictly speaking, events are only events. It is the attitude we take toward them that turns them into a comedy or a tragedy. Arwin can decide that he is a victim or he can take control of the situation. If he is lucky, he'll realize that he lives in a world where everything is completely relative."

"Which literary genre do you think he'll choose?" Dhimas' fingers hovered above the keyboard. He was getting ready.

They both looked at each other.

FERRÉ

Because Rana was out of town on an assignment, he was able to talk to her before going to bed. After even a short conversation—ten minutes or so—he was able to sleep through the night with a smile on his lips.

"How is it going, Princess? You sound happy. It must be great meeting all those celebrities."

"Don't tease me. You know how much I hate going to these pretentious award nights. But at least they give me an excuse now."

"Oh. Have you met anyone interesting?"

"If you mean what I think you mean, the answer is 'No, of course not,'" Rana laughed. "But I can relax at this sort of event, watch what is happening, telephone you."

Her words caught him fair and square. To have her call him at the end of the day was very precious and very complicated. It required an annual award program and for the top editor to approve her covering it. Which meant that, in the final scheme of things, he was no one. His bitterness reared within him like a poisonous snake.

> *This is wrong! Why can't we change things? Why do you*
> *have to live like that, Rana? Why do I have to live like*
> *this? Why do I feel like this? I feel so totally lost.*
> *It's so irrational. It's killing me!*

Ferré struggled to hold back the words. They were there inside him all the time, but he could never say them because they would hurt Rana.

She was suffering too.

> *Suffering? She had everything: a husband she couldn't*
> *leave without shocking society and a secret lover*
> *who loved her half to death.*

> *A pair of fancy shoes that pinched when she wore them*
> *and a comfortable pair of slippers in the closet.*

> *How are you, Slippers? Do you like it there,*
> *thrown away in the back of the dark closet,*
> *where nobody can see you?*

Ferré couldn't restrain the renegade thoughts that were running through his brain. Unaware, Rana continued to chatter: "And can you imagine, everyone thought I was talking to Arwin. They said we sounded so in love." She laughed again.

> *Teach me to be as naïve as you. Show me how to laugh.*
> *How to be happy in our world together. The pain is*
> *almost more than I can bear. Or teach me how to lie like*
> *you do, when you hurt and laugh at the same time.*

"That isn't funny, Princess," he said coldly.

Her laughter froze. "I wanted to tell them it was you, Ferré. You, you." Her voice trailed off. The word "you" continued to echo inside her heart.

Ferré could not reply. He was very angry.

I'm tired, Princess.

That night he could not sleep with a smile on his lips. He sat in his study, sorting through his scraps of paper, trying to gather the scattered fragments of his love together; trying to feel the ecstasy he had known with Rana; trying to be strong when he knew that it made no sense. Ferré was in his world of simulacra, the last refuge available to him in the torment of his inner conflict.

Arwin

The hotel car park, two o'clock in the afternoon. Two people stood face to face, their focus on nothing else but each other. Despite the precautions they took not to be seen, it was impossible not to see them. They were so obvious. So unaware of everyone and everything else. *How could they see anything else? They were so in love. So madly in love.*

Arwin sat in the car, unable to think. Staring at that one point. His thoughts were like a beam of light passing through a crystal and shooting off in a million different directions. He tried to decide, to find a solution, to work out what he should do. And he couldn't. Nothing came to him.

Anyone could see what he saw. The sweet face of his wife, open like the most beautiful flower he could imagine. So sweet it was like insulin racing through his veins. He was afraid that if he looked at her much longer, he would contract diabetes. She was so... *happy.*

He couldn't feel hatred for Rana. Or for the man. Only enormous hatred for himself.

I've never deserved to have her. I've known that for years, but I've never admitted it. What a selfish fool I've been. I've never been able to make Rana shine with happiness like that. I thought I really loved her, but I was only stopping her from being happy. Forgive me, Rana. I did what I could. I only wish I could have done more.

DHIMAS AND RUBEN

"Amazing," Ruben sighed. "I didn't think he'd be like that."

"He really does love his wife. At a certain point, love can destroy our own petty ego. If his wife is happy, he's happy. If she is sad, he is too."

"And he takes full responsibility for how he feels."

"He does. Most people spend their time blaming everyone else."

"Can love really be so magnificent?" Ruben wondered. "I could talk about the theory all day long, but if I was in his situation, I don't think I'd be so generous. He accepts his wife and her love for another man as well."

"So can you imagine how big a heart it takes to love the whole world?"

"As big as love itself."

15

In Love

Each morning, Diva followed the same ritual. First she went to a traditional market. The most she ever brought home was a few small plastic bags containing fruit or cakes. What she most enjoyed was looking at the piles of fruit and vegetables. Just looking. She would sit for a long time in a corner of the market, smiling to herself.

From there she went straight to a kindergarten. She knew exactly when the children come out to play. She would sit on a bench outside the fence surrounding the playground and watch the children, smiling to herself.

Finally, before returning home, she would visit the flower stalls by the roadside. Diva knew some of the sellers well and they allowed her to sit on their wooden benches. Sometimes she took home a bag containing plants or a few packets of fertilizer. Sometimes she took nothing home at all. She simply wanted to be there. Watching. And smiling to herself.

Today, as she finished her breakfast, preparing for her ritual stroll, she glanced out her window.

Suddenly a man emerged from the house across the road. Diva curled her lips in scorn. It was only half past eight, but he already had his cellphone pressed against his ear. He was speaking very quickly. His tie hung, waiting to be knotted; a sharp crease down the front of his trousers, as straight as a die. His black leather briefcase would still have looked expensive if it were a million miles away.

She knew the type well: guys who always had wise-ass nicknames for their bosses—"The Fat Chinaman," "Pot-Bellied Honky," "Big-Mouthed Jap"—and who would laugh about them at lunch, before meekly going back to the office with their heads bowed, like chickens scratching for worms. Her nights were filled with men like this.

Disgusted, Diva turned away. The man was pure visual pollution. But then, suddenly, something changed. The man stopped everything he was doing. His face completely relaxed. The tension was gone. He spoke slowly, enjoying every word, as if they were precious pearls. His eyes gazed into the distance, looking at nothing at all. But no. He was looking at love. No matter where his eyes turned, he saw only love.

Diva began to smile. *The man was in love.* So very much in love. He seemed to be turning into love itself. His smile, the expression on his face, the way he held his cellphone, every movement he made. Diva held her breath. Time stopped flowing. Instead it fell on her mind like dew.

Drop... by drop...

by drop...

b...y d...r...o...p...

Everything seemed to move in s l o o o w

m m m o o o t i o n n.

Moments like this could move her to prayer. To pray that for a brief moment the world might slow down, that everything might gain a new self-image, filled with meaning: the muscles in the leg as they stretched during the act of running; the tongue as it curled in a kiss; the fingers as they quivered on touching the hand of the lover; a lock of hair as it danced in the wind; the corner of the mouth as a smile formed.... Then each wrinkle would find its true meaning;

each hurried sentence would be important; and any face that tried to tell a lie would blush with shame.

Nothing is more beautiful than an act performed in a slow motion. Diva touched the window. She wanted to feel the whole scene. If she could, she would have said to him: *Please don't go. Stay there, oh man in love.*

But the Invisible Hand flicked the switch and time began again. The man snapped his phone shut and turned back into a businessman. He rushed to his car and sped away, back to the front line.

For a moment, Diva felt very alone.

Ferré

Saturday night. Ferré was at loose ends. Disgusted with himself and unable to pretend any longer that he had anything that might keep him busy at home, he had decided to spend the evening with Rafael and his girlfriend, Lala. They took one car, ate at a restaurant together, and then went to watch a movie together.

The queue for tickets outside the theater snaked like a Chinese New Year procession.

"You two find somewhere to wait," Ferré offered. "Or go for a walk."

"That's alright," Lala immediately replied. "We're in this together, Ferré."

"Just a minute!" Rafael interrupted. "Why do you think we brought him along? He can stand in line while we go off somewhere together. He has to be good for something!"

"Scram! Get out of here!" said Ferré, laughing.

Rafael joined in the laughter.

Ferré watched the couple as they walked away. He saw Rafael put his arm around Lala's waist and watched as Lala rested her head on Rafael's shoulder. Side by side, they glided away, as if they were walking on a thick carpet.

Looking around he saw another couple holding hands. Their palms seemed to be glued together. He saw another man waiting to buy a ticket, his arms around his girlfriend's waist as she moved in front of him. A woman fed her boyfriend a cream puff as he played "Time Crisis." Another man waited patiently outside the women's restroom. As soon as his girlfriend appeared, his eyes lit up, as though he had just seen an angel emerge from a heavenly lotus.

Had the story been different, Ferré was sure that he and Rana would have won first prize for the way they walked. The carpet would have been so thick people would have had to crane their necks to see them. Even Cupid wouldn't have bothered wasting his arrows on them.

If only I could say that I had been lucky, lucky enough
to have met you two years and forty-three days ago,
before you married him.

Later that night, as Rafael drove him home, Ferré asked: "Do you always take the women you're dating to the movies?" He was still thinking about what he had seen.

"Isn't that what everyone does?" Rafael laughed. "A necessary first step, the prelude. You should do a survey. I'm sure most couples in this far-flung nation started out in exactly that way."

"It has never seemed like a big deal before. I just want to be like everyone else. You know, to be able to go out to the movies on Saturday night and to my arms around my girlfriend's shoulders while we're queuing for tickets, or at least hold her hand. That's all. Without worrying about who is behind us, or having to look around all the time; without hurrying away when I see someone I know coming towards us."

Rafael knew where the conversation was heading. "Hey, Ferré…"

"Stop! I'm not asking for your pity!" Ferré exclaimed.

"Pity? You were stupid enough to get yourself into this," Rafael replied. "I don't have any pity for you. I don't even feel sorry for you, so you needn't worry about that. If anything, I am concerned about your sanity. You're a highly intelligent man and, the way I see it, you could go over the edge if you're not careful. Do you understand what I'm saying?"

Ferré said nothing. He realized that his friend's words could indeed come true.

I'm a man who lives by numbers. Our numbers are not good, Princess. I'm a man who needs to be recognized. No one recognizes who we are.

He remembered earlier that night, when Rafael came to pick him up. Before his friend had arrived, Ferré was busy scanning the TV listings, trying to find out what time a particular soap opera came on. Today's episode was about a woman with two lovers. Tomorrow's was about a man with two women. It was all getting very exciting. The characters were utterly confused. They didn't know who they should choose. Ferré watched the series regularly, scarcely blinking the whole time.

There was a pile of magazines on his sofa with colored stickers marking a story, an article, a novelette, a medical column, which dealt with the destructive effects of an outsider on an established marriage.

Once he would have dismissed all of this as garbage, people turning their lives into melodramas, trying to escape their ordinary reality by overdosing on tragedy. Now, however, he sympathized completely with the stories and the people in them. Everything he read, heard, and saw, including Rafael's curses and abuse, told him that he would inevitably lose. Society and his own sense of guilt would sooner or later defeat him. He would always be "the trouble-maker." There were other names too: idiot, the other man, victim of a passing infatuation....

When the bell rang, Ferré covered the magazines with a cushion, and ran to open the door. Half way there, he remembered something else: to change the channel.

When Ferré opened the door, Rafael greeted him with a loud laugh. "When did you start watching the soaps?"

"What soaps?" Ferré responded indignantly.

"Sure, your television is on CNN now. But," Rafael chuckled again, "I've been standing out here for the last five minutes. You're in a bad way, my friend. If it was possible to inject some sense into you, I'd send you off to the emergency ward at once."

"I only watched for a few minutes. It doesn't mean anything," Ferré lied. Then, in a slightly louder voice, he asked, "Why would I watch that sort of program anyway?" *Yes, why indeed?*

Life's whole journey is worse than any film, Princess.
The blood is real. So are the tears. You can't use a double
to escape the pain.

Ferré pushed his thoughts aside and returned to the present. Quickly he looked out of Rafael's car. They were stopped at a red light.

A motorcycle pulled up on the left. An old, small motorcycle, made during the 1970s, its headlight as pale as a kerosene lantern in a roadside stall. The driver was a young man with a thick moustache. His helmet looked like a bucket. He wasn't particularly handsome, but there was a glow in his eyes. The woman sitting behind him wasn't particularly beautiful either. She wore an undistinguished blouse, covered with a tiny floral pattern. Her long hair was gathered in a clip behind her head. She also wore a jacket, to ward off the cold. It was too big to be hers. The jacket obviously belonged to the man. Their faces shone with a steady glow. The flames of love had settled into a bright, ongoing light, free from sudden unexpected flare-ups. Perhaps they were hoping to have their first child this year.

Ferré's brief composure was shattered.

He looked across the road, at a couple waiting for one of the last buses of the night. They had no car, no motorcycle. *But look at her face.* The woman clung tightly to her man's arm. Her face was full of trust. With him to hold onto, she didn't mind the cold or the endless waiting.

> *What is this? A supermarket of love? Overstocked? All*
> *goods must go? I don't want anything complicated. I'd*
> *settle for the simple brand.*
> *I don't need the old-fashioned kind.*

But he was born with expensive tastes. The sale was all around him and he could only watch others walk where he could only dream of being. Ferré sat back in his seat, his forehead marked with a big sign that said: "You can look but you mustn't touch."

16

Tears

The rehearsal for the fashion show was proceeding. "One, two, three, four!" the choreographer shouted. "Let's go! Oh, cut! Cut! Wanda, Henny... a little bit faster, ladies. Again!"

Diva sat at the edge of the stage, massaging her heel. She watched Adi as he unconsciously navigated the rehearsal space, calling out commands to the models.

Crash! One of the models fell directly in front of her. Some onlookers moaned, others laughed.

Diva was one of the people who laughed but she quickly helped the girl to her feet. "They're only ten centimeters high, but they do hurt, don't they?" Diva giggled. "Or did you hurt your dignity?"

The girl didn't know whether to complain or just thank Diva for helping her.

"Why do you have to be so rude?" said a model standing next to Diva. "Have some pity on the poor girl."

Diva turned around. "I didn't notice you rushing to help her."

A mixture of expressions crossed the woman's face. "You are such a bitch!" she finally replied angrily. "Do you think that it is funny falling down in high heels?"

Diva looked at her in wonder. "You were the first one to laugh. And you laughed louder than anyone else."

"What's your problem?" Furious, the model stalked away.

"Diva only has one problem," Risty retorted, to a chorus of giggles. "She never feels sorry for anyone."

It was true. Diva never felt sorry for anyone. While there were limits to how high a heel could be, there were no limits to the heights of human arrogance. And there was no limit to the amount of meaningless admiration some people craved; people who had nothing more to offer than a beautiful body or a gorgeous, but expressionless, face; people who derived self-importance from a forty-story office block, their credit flow, or an academic title that could dazzle the foolish; people who needed something that made them feel superior to everyone else. She didn't feel sorry for any of them. They were monkeys climbing the corporate tree: the higher they got, the more their brains shriveled. What would it be like to fall from such heights? Diva frowned. She was tired.

The real question was why she had to witness such stupidity. And why couldn't anyone else see it? Why was she the only person who truly wanted to live?

She yearned for her tiny garden.

"Diva, come on!" Adi's shrill voice startled her. "Let's take it from the top. Start walking with the opening song. Hup, hup!"

"Adi, I'm not feeling well. Can I go home? I'll be there tomorrow night."

Adi was mildly surprised. *She must be really sick*, he thought to himself. Diva never missed a rehearsal, even though that wouldn't be a problem for a model of her caliber. He felt he had no other choice but to let her go.

In fact, Diva was sick. Her weariness was a symptom of something far more serious than influenza or smallpox. At moments like this, she wanted to lash out and hit everyone, and to hug them at the same time. To tell them how disappointed she was and how much she loved them.

"Ahmad, take me home, please."

"Yes, Miss."

In the rear-view mirror, Ahmad glanced at his boss: her beautiful face looked strangely sad. He had worked for Diva for over four years. During that time, she had almost always traveled alone. She had certainly never taken anyone home with her. As they drove the city streets, she spent part of the time talking on her cellphone and the rest staring out the window in silence, occasionally biting her lower lip. Although she was not the sort of person who talked a lot or made jokes, he knew that she cared about him. She had never given him new clothes at the end of the fasting month or shared in the communal slaughter of a cow on ritual days. Yet she had paid tuition for his children's school, as well as fees for additional courses. She made sure that they had all the books they needed. Diva had helped his wife learn to sew, so that she could set up her own small business. She had ordered the couple to set up a small lending library for the children in their neighborhood. And covered all their living expenses.

His boss had once told him: "If I only paid you a salary and I suddenly lost all my money tomorrow and had to let you go, you wouldn't have anything to live on until you found someone else to employ you. I want you to be able to fend for yourself, even without me. Without any boss at all. I don't want you to worry about how you'll pay for this or that. Your children won't be able to be at the top of their classes if their stomachs are always playing the rumba, if they don't have pens and pencils or the right books. You need to keep your house neat and decorate it with a few flower pots. And boil the drinking water."

Diva was a strange boss. She really worried about things he didn't worry about. She was concerned. It was a blessing to be able to work for her. Quietly he sneaked a second look in the rear-view mirror. His boss was crying, silently weeping. He could see the tears flowing down her cheeks without a sound. Ahmad was deeply moved, yet he didn't know what he could do other than keep driving.

Dressed in a long white t-shirt and a pair of shorts, Diva sat in her bedroom, facing the window. There was nothing she could do, except hug the throw pillow in her arms and cry. She wanted to let out her weariness. Her body was still sensitive enough to tell her that she couldn't bear this any longer, she needed to cry.

The pain hurt immensely. It made her sob and gasp, until she was completely exhausted. But she had to go through to the end, until she was washed clean, until she had been thoroughly *purified*. God had not created her to bear other people's stupidity.

FERRÉ

Even after he arrived home, Ferré couldn't stop thinking. Long after he should have been in bed, he still sat lost in thought. Why were he and Rana so different from everyone else?

He had everything. His woman would never need to ride on the back of a dilapidated motorcycle, soaked by the rain. They would never need to walk through the savage Jakarta night in order to wait for a bus. But he and Rana would never know the peace those couples knew, the strength with which they faced their lives.

A gust of wind swept past Ferré, startling him. The sound was as plaintive as the gentle melody of a bamboo flute. Quickly he rose to his feet and closed the window. He had lived in this house for three years and had never known a wind like that before.

How strange, he thought. The wind hadn't disturbed anything. Ferré looked up at the trees. The leaves were scarcely moving. But the miraculous wind had led his eyes to look at a window in the house across the road. He could see through the window a woman, sitting with her knees curled up beneath her chin and her head half bowed. She was beautiful. Framed by the stars in the night sky, she looked almost surreal. It was like a painting. The whole scene was exquisite. Ferré watched, spellbound.

One minute after another passed by without his noticing. For a very long time, neither Ferré nor the image moved.

Finally, the subject of the painting raised her head. Perhaps she wanted to look at the sky. The street light shone directly onto the beautiful face, highlighting the tears flowing down her cheeks. The picture was even more perfect. Carefully Ferré noted the woman's eyes. They were staring at something.

Slowly he followed the direction of her gaze. The painting changed into a vast expanse of stars. Ferré gasped. He could hardly believe what he was seeing.

He had looked at the sky a thousand times. He had called her name a thousand times. Tonight he had at last met her: *the Falling Star*. She had sped by him so quickly and was so overwhelmingly attractive. Ferré was stunned.

Catching his breath, he looked back at the window… and was disappointed. She had closed the curtains and vanished.

Slowly Ferré moved away from his own window. He felt a million and one emotions. For years he had searched for his enemy. He had never expected her to be so lovely or so astonishing.

DHIMAS AND RUBEN

Dhimas was overwhelmed. Half of what he felt would have been more than both of them could have dealt with.

"They have finally met," he whispered.

"And what are you going to do with them now?" Ruben asked, as he stood behind him with a cup of coffee in his hand. He was consumed with curiosity.

"I don't know!" Dhimas replied. "I really don't!"

17

The Two Greatest Idiots
of the Twenty-First Century

Rana had not talked with this particular woman for a long time. Her own mother. Really talked, not just exchanged routine pleasantries: "How are you?" "How was the test, positive or negative?" "When can we go shopping at the mall?" "There is a special sale at the Metro. Will you drive me?" "Darling, could you come to Bandung with me? I'd like to go shopping at one of the factory outlets and bring back some of those brownies and cream puffs that your father-in-law enjoys so very much."

"What is it, Rana?" she asked, once she realized that her daughter had been staring at her for a long time.

"I need to talk to you, Mom. It's about Arwin." Rana swallowed hard.

"Is there some problem? Nothing to do with a baby, is it?"

"No, it might be connected, but no, it isn't really," Rana was confused. This was much more difficult than she had expected.

"Have you had a fight?" her mother prodded. "Is Arwin up to something you don't like?"

"I just wanted to ask you something," Rana said cautiously. "You and Dad have been married for a long time. Have you ever felt bored or that something was missing in your relationship?"

"Oh, is that all?" her mother interrupted. Her face relaxed immediately. "Boredom is a natural part of any marriage; the important thing is knowing what to do about it. There's nothing to worry about."

Rana wasn't sure that her mother understood what she was asking. "I don't just mean bored. It is more like... Something is wrong, something is missing, something is happening that shouldn't be happening." She said the words slowly, emphatically.

"Do you mean you wish you hadn't married Arwin? Is that it?"

"Have you ever regretted marrying Dad, even once, in your whole life?"

"There's nothing wrong with Arwin. He's a good man, responsible, pious, he has a good job, he comes from a good family."

"That wasn't what I asked you."

This time her mother waited before she replied. She struggled to understand Rana's question and to formulate the appropriate answer. "Every marriage has its ups and downs, like most things in this world. But with marriage, you can't shrug your shoulders and throw away the bits you don't want. A good wife realizes that her husband is not perfect. You both need to acknowledge the other's shortcomings and forgive them every single day. The key to a happy marriage is good communication. And never try to resolve something while you're still angry."

Rana felt as though they were talking on two different levels. She hadn't come for this sort of advice. The magazines were full of "tips for a happy marriage" and "words to the weary." The woman's words were part of the standard marriage first-aid kit which belonged in every home. She didn't need that. It would take more than a trip to the medicine cabinet to fix what ailed her. Rana was ready for the Intensive Care Unit.

"Are you happy, Mom?" she asked. "Have you always been happy?"

"Of course, dear. What sort of a question is that? I'm happy that you and your sisters have grown up to be such fine people. You've all made good marriages. What more could I want?"

Despite the certainty in her mother's voice, Rana was still not satisfied. "I don't mean that. I mean something more, something beyond your children. Are you—personally, as an individual, within yourself —really happy in your marriage?" Rana's words were deliberate.

Eventually the woman smiled. "Now I understand what you mean," she gently replied. "One day, after you've been married for ten or fifteen years, you'll know the answer to your question. You'll understand happiness differently then. Can you see what I'm saying? There will come a time when your own personal happiness isn't so important any more."

That's it! Rana shouted to herself. At a certain point, people turned into something else. One became a mutant, no longer capable of being oneself. She had seen it happen so many times. The woman she was talking with was no longer Raden Ajeng Widya Purwaningrum Sastrodhinoto. Rana couldn't tell who she was. All Rana knew was that the woman was a Wife. Married to a certain Man. The Mother of certain Children, called A, B and C.

The happiness I want will turn into a different sort of happiness. At a certain point I want to dissolve into a new and different person. Other people will forget about this Rana. Even I will forget about her. Which Rana do I want to be? Is there still time?

Rana looked at her mother and suddenly saw a multitude of faces, linked like chains about her. Her heart stopped beating for a moment. Rana realized that she herself had begun to mutate. The chains were starting to form around her too and she didn't know how to shed them. Could she, should she, let go? Would it be right to do so, would it be wrong? Again her heart stopped beating.

FERRÉ

Sometimes the Poet was silent. Now and then the homunculus in his brain lost all interest in writing and went on strike. So he took out his frustration on Rafael instead.

"I miss the good old-fashioned days," Ferré lamented, following what was by now a well-established script. "You know, having dinner at a fine restaurant with a table for two. Exchanging birthday presents and so on. But I couldn't even bring myself to enter her house."

Rafael, on the other hand, had no poetic sensibility. He enjoyed abusing Ferré. "How does your head feel now?" he shouted. "I bet it's much lighter than it used to be. Ever since you fell in love, your brain seems to have shrunk to the size of a pea. The very idea of going to her house was absolutely stupid, you poor bastard!"

"She suggested I bring you with me," Ferré smiled.

"What?" Rafael guffawed. "Just imagine turning up at her house! Ladies and gentlemen, please welcome Ferré and Rafael, the two greatest idiots of the twenty-first century."

"Would you please cut the official ribbon, Mr Rafael."

"Gong!"

Their hands met in a high five, then the two men fell backwards, laughing uncontrollably. Two boys freed from the constraint of their adult male bodies.

Rafael lazily flicked the curtain back and forth. "Wow!" he said, as he stared out the window. "That's the sort of babe who could turn me into an idiot any time she liked."

Ferré followed his gaze. The motor of the silver sedan had just turned on. A woman walked to the car and slid into the back seat.

Rafael purred. "Rana might be as sweet as candy. But why not look closer to home? You've got a whole candy factory right before your very eyes and you can't even see it."

"It is weird," Ferré was forced to agree.

"Where have you been all this time?"

Ferré thought about the question. Perhaps Rafael was right. He lived in a luxurious house but he was never really home.

Rafael sighed, breaking Ferré's train of thought. "Imagine if I didn't have Lala and had a couple thousand dollars to splurge."

"I don't get you."

Rafael looked at Ferré in disbelief, then laughed. "You really don't know who your neighbor is, do you?"

"No. Do you?" Ferré asked innocently.

"Heavenly Father, forgive our dear friend. He is so stupid," Rafael wailed. "Listen to me. The chick is our nation's supermodel. Crème de la crème. Her name is Diva. And she's ready stock, man. As long as you have, mmm, perhaps fifteen hundred to two thousand dollars. Maybe more."

"Are you serious?"

"I don't know all the details. Whether that is the short-term rate, the long-term rate, one hit, a session, twenty-four hours. All I know is she charges in dollars and since the economy collapsed she has adjusted her tariff accordingly. Before the monetary crisis, I heard that some guys were prepared to put out five to six thousand for the privilege."

"How do you know all that?"

"Because I'm not like you: a total nerd who spends all his time working," Rafael grinned. "But then who one day goes completely crazy and falls deeply in love with another man's wife."

"Shut up!"

Rafael suddenly became serious. "You know, Ferré, I'll never agree with you about this but I'll never stop being your friend either. You can be sure of that. No matter what idiotic thing you decide to do."

"Yeah, the two greatest idiots of the twenty-first century!"

"Just one," Rafael corrected him. "But I'll join the idiot-army to keep you company."

Moments like this made Ferré think again about the nature of Love. Why shouldn't he and Rafael marry each other? They were completely and unconditionally loyal to each other. They gave each other total freedom to lead their lives the way they wanted. They didn't need to live under the one roof. They didn't need to share a common budget. And Ferré was convinced that his friendship with Rafael would stand the test of time.

How did other people live out their love? They pretended that it was the basis of a grand and glorious institution called *marriage*. Why were they so eager to dominate each other, fighting like deranged mining companies to claim some tiny plot of land? Could the grandeur of love be contained in half-acre blocks? What was it all about? A legalization of lust? A permit to sleep together? Another statistic on the census form? The state intruding on people's lives? What was commitment all about? Why did people need to make promises to each other?

Ferré felt suddenly very strange, totally bewildered.

"Hey, what's happening to you, Ferré?"

"Call me crazy if you like, but I think I'm about to propose to you."

"You're a psycho," Rafael replied, nodding insistently. "I think I'd better get out of here. Bye!"

Rafael scampered out the front door.

Dhimas and Ruben

"Can you feel it?"

"Yes. We've almost reached your point of bifurcation. All it requires is a little more turbulence."

"Soon the quantum leap will be their favorite sport."

The two men sat back comfortably in their chairs.

"Don't tell me you need to make more coffee," Dhimas exclaimed as soon as he noticed Ruben's increasing restlessness.

"And don't tell me that you're going to read that same magazine again," Ruben replied defiantly.

"Well, why shouldn't I? There's nothing else worth reading here. It's appalling." Dhimas continued flicking through the pages of the journal. "Much longer and I'll know the whole thing by heart."

"I'll test you," Ruben said lazily. "What's on page 107?"

"Get a life," exclaimed Dhimas. "That's too easy."

"OK, OK. I'll ask you something else. Something much harder." Ruben refused to give in. He enjoyed teasing Dhimas. "Tell me the name of the model on the front cover."

"Now that I do know. Her name is Diva. Everyone knows that: except you, of course."

"I don't care. She's not the president." Ruben shrugged, apparently indifferent to Dhimas' taunt. Inwardly he wondered if he really was as blind as everyone suggested.

"She's pretty, isn't she!"

Ruben giggled. "If she was interested in you, you'd soon become a heterosexual, wouldn't you?"

"Maybe," Dhimas grinned. "Would you?"

"Never," Ruben said in a rather unconvincing voice.

"Really?"

"Well, maybe... if she was as clever and intriguing as the Falling Star," Ruben added shyly.

"This is getting serious. Soon we might have to stop being gay."

RANA

Gita studied Rana's troubled face. They had been friends since high school and she had never seen Rana in such a state. Rana used to be so strong and confident. Now their meetings always ended with a runny nose and red, swollen eyes.

"I keep having these pains in my chest," Rana sighed.

"That is because you're under so much stress. You should have known that falling in love is bad for your health."

Rana gave a broad smile. "As if I had any choice in the matter."

"Divorce is no easy matter, Rana."

"I wouldn't ask Arwin for anything. I just want him to let me go." She began to cry again.

"As far as money is concerned, I'm sure that your Ferré is perfectly capable of looking after you. But are you ready for the consequences? To face your family, Arwin's family, the people at work, everyone else. Ferré is a public figure. You know that." Gita paused for a moment, then continued with her list, "And Arwin's family are aristocrats. Their good name means everything to them."

"Ferré has never said anything about this, but I know it could do considerable damage to his reputation."

"How would your family treat you afterwards? Have you thought about that?" Gita's list seemed never ending.

Rana began to feel cornered. Staring into the distance, she said: "I think I'll just run away, disappear."

"Where will you go? Timbuktu?"

"That's not far enough."

There was the whole planet to choose from. It wouldn't be hard. Somewhere like Gili Terawangan off the island of Lombok would do. A beach somewhere, pretty as a postcard. Or a snow-covered mountain. A large tropical park with rivers and a waterfall. A house somewhere, large enough so that she and Ferré wouldn't get bored with each other, and they could make love wherever they wanted. No more pretending. No more doing what other people wanted. Free of all the rules and regulations that enchained them.

That would be paradise. Something she used to believe in a long time ago and which Ferré had taught her to believe in again. Ferré was a sort of alien, a creature who had dropped from the sky and shown her how narrow and boring her world was. Unfortunately, Rana wasn't sure if she could live with him on his planet without hurting a lot of other people. But neither was she willing to say goodbye to all her dreams.

Gita felt that the time had come to do something. Her fingers quickly searched through her bag. "Rana," she said cautiously, "I have something for you."

Gita pulled out a piece of paper and a ballpoint pen. She was writing something.

Rana deeply sighed, "Gita, I don't need to go to a therapist, a marriage counselor or anyone like that."

"No. That wasn't what I had in mind. Not at all." Gita shook her head. "I'm not sure how I would classify this person. You'd better find out for yourself. But he—or she—just might be able to help you."

"Who?" Rana still did not understand.

"Supernova."

18

Cyber Avatar

The two men lay back and stared at the bedroom ceiling. Who knows how long they had been there. They were utterly confused.

"It is time our avatar appeared, Ruben."

"I know, I know."

There was no simple solution to the problem.

"I think I need another cup of coffee," Ruben exclaimed as he struggled off the bed.

"Just a minute!" Dhimas insisted. "We can't do anything else until we've worked this out."

"Give up, Dhimas. This is all too hard. Admit it: we've reached a dead end. Once we admit that, then maybe an idea will come."

Reluctantly Dhimas finally allowed Ruben to slip away to the kitchen, into the arms of his second lover: caffeine.

"It is not easy creating an avatar," Ruben called out from the kitchen. "The other characters were easy by comparison."

"There's no need to teach your grandmother to suck eggs, you know," Dhimas grumbled softly.

"The avatar of the twenty-first century won't appear riding on a donkey, dressed in a long white robe, or wearing Aladdin's slippers. He won't have a long beard down to his waist. Our avatar should enjoy meeting people. He should go to the movies, watch films and television, own a computer."

"Eat at McDonalds."

"Go to the mall."

"Play games at Time Zone."

"That might be a bit extreme."

"Practice a modern form of asceticism and not live in a remote cave."

"Right. He shouldn't be some skinny old guy who spends half his life sitting around like a statue." Ruben stirred his coffee one last time before beginning to drink it. Suddenly he stopped, fascinated by the coffee grounds whirling around in his cup. A non-local signal had switched on a light bulb in his head. He had an idea!

"I know!" he shouted from the kitchen. Bounding out, he found Dhimas already sitting in the study, eager to learn what he had discovered.

Ruben's face shone like a xenon lamp. Firmly he said: "He is... a cyber avatar."

Supernova

The monitor glowed as the hands again danced across the keyboard. One after another, the thoughts began to take shape.

SUPERNOVA

– For those who want to LIVE –

Welcome.

Today I want to talk about something called "recto-verso."

Recto-verso occurs when two figures on the opposite sides of a piece of paper, recto and verso, combine to form one whole picture. A simple example is the icon on our banknotes.

Imagine a circle containing five petals radiating from a central dot. Three petals are printed on one side of the paper. A circle and the other two petals are on the other side. Only when you see both sides together do you become aware of the full circle, the five petals and the dot in the middle.

Because we usually don't see things as one complete whole, we don't realize that we are recto-versal. Too many people spend their days feeling miserable because they feel incomplete but can't work out what is missing from their lives. So they search and search outside of their own essential nature until finally they are completely lost. They struggle in various ways, mentally and physically, to define that missing "something," which they usually think exists in the "external" world.

Human beings were created for only one purpose: to discover their own true nature. When they regain that wholeness, they stop feeling small and insignificant, lost in a vast universe.

What if our sense of our own completeness could be achieved through a simple act of recto-verso? That would mean we didn't need to look anywhere else. It would mean that we could regain our completeness just by changing our perspective. If we step back from the broken pieces of our own mind, then we can see the whole picture. This means yet again (and again) that what we are seeking does not exist outside ourselves. On the contrary, it is very close. It is inseparable from who we really are. Find the button and push it. Look at things differently.

Stop feeling miserable. Stop feeling that you need help in order to be whole. Stop calling out to something a long way off. Stop acting like the fish swimming all over the sea in search of water. You already have everything you need.

No one else can give you that wholeness. You are already full; no one can add anything to who you are. No one and nothing can separate you from your own intrinsic nature.

It all depends on whether or not you're prepared to be aware of this basic truth.

Find the button and push it.

We will meet again when the silver threads come together once more.

<send>

DHIMAS AND RUBEN

"That's it? Our avatar preaches over the internet?"

"Preaches? This is much more than preaching. Supernova is a form of turbulence people can access whenever and wherever they want; one capable of amplifying their understanding in a non-hierarchical manner, beyond all institutions and dogmas; completely and totally non-linear. Plus, the internet recognizes no territorial boundaries. It's just perfect, wouldn't you agree?"

"Our avatar can carry out *The Aquarian Conspiracy* over the Web."

"Precisely. Naisbitt and Toffler predicted that this would one day be the most efficient system available," Ruben said, nodding to himself. From the start, chaos theory had allowed him to move away from scientific predictability and to reject all hierarchies. It taught him that each element in a system is as important as every other element. Even though those elements are interconnected, each has the potential to develop in its own particular manner.

Ruben was again reminded that the same applies to our nervous system, which is a series of random fibers linked by particular molecules. Through the process of feedback, the molecules can bring the fibers together so that they link up with each other. Remarkably, no pair of fibers ever joins together in exactly the same way. Being individuals, they organize themselves in the way they themselves want, even while remaining part of the wider network. People are beginning to realize that our social and economic systems behave in the same way. In the future, chaos will be the key to effective management; non-linear business environments will give employees creative roles in discovering more efficient ways of working. Amnesty International and Greenpeace are two examples of highly effective global networks which are not constrained by state borders or social hierarchies. In fact, many people believe that in the future, governments will consist of a vast series of multi-dimensional networks. These networks will provide citizens with a wide range of choices, through which individuals will participate in the control of their own worlds, each according to her capabilities and interests.

"Ruben, does this mean that the avatar is a virtual person?"

Ruben returned the question to Dhimas. "I don't know. What do you think?"

"I want him to be a real person," Dhimas said with quiet intensity. "I want him to be able to reach out and touch each of their lives directly. So that, without their realizing it, they all reflect each other."

RANA

Each night for the past few weeks, Rana had perched in front of her computer screen, reading the comments and drawing strength from them.

At first, she suspected that she had logged on to the ravings of a madman. Perhaps the Webmaster was a psychopath, with the terrifying ability to turn everything she had formerly known upside down. Gradually, however, Rana had come to feel that the world was mad and that Supernova was the only sane person she knew.

Slowly the messages became like oases in a desert: They refreshed her, made her laugh, made her cry out with pain, and sometimes knocked her right off her stool. Day by day she began to see the world differently.

She was also frustrated. Rana sent several messages to Supernova, but never received a reply. Perhaps she didn't know how to ask properly. Perhaps Supernova was so high and mighty that Rana's poor little questions didn't count.

> Supernova, I really like what you have to say. Would you mind if I told you a little about myself? I'm a woman, age 28, the wife of a kind and successful man. At first glance, there is nothing wrong with our marriage. But a few months ago, I met another man and we fell in love. He is the most extraordinary man I've ever known. More than that. He's the RIGHT man for me. If you know what I mean. He isn't perfect, but then neither am I or my husband. But he's like the piece of a jigsaw puzzle that fits precisely into the empty space.
>
> We want to be together, which means that I would have to request a divorce from my husband. And that would be very difficult. My husband comes from a traditional family of aristocrats. They are pillars of society. Everyone expects them to set a high moral example to the rest of the community. The very idea of divorce would strike them as utterly shameful.

Rana wrote down five more points and sent them off. There was no reply.

Supernova, I really like what you have to say. I have a slight problem and I'm sure you could help me. The thing is that I'm married but I've fallen in love with someone else. Have I done something wrong? I'd just like to know what you think. That's all.

No reply.

Supernova, imagine you were married and one day you met another man or woman and fell in love. Would you leave your husband or wife to be with him?

It was such a stupid question that Rana didn't even send it. Surely such a thing would never happen to Supernova. Such a problem would hardly matter at the level Supernova lived.

Supernova, I've made a lot of decisions in my life without knowing who I really am. Now that I do know, is it right to destroy everything I have worked so hard to achieve? To break the promises I made, forget about my responsibilities, and ignore the consequences of my past actions; all for the sake of some new dream that will hurt many other people? Or should I stay where I am, and accept all of this as part of the learning process?

No reply.

Supernova, I want to go back to when I was a girl, to make up for my mistakes. I want to change my destiny. I'm sorry I was never brave enough to make my own decisions. I want to know who I am. I want to be free to love the way that is best for me. Please help me....

No reply.

Supernova, are you there? You never reply to any of my letters.

Still no reply.

Rana was furious. Despite all the beautiful slogans, maybe this psychopath was only interested in the really big problems: basic human rights, the global economy, the ecology, that sort of thing. Rana, with her tiny problems, was totally unimportant. "Rubbish!" she growled. Supernova, she decided, took a delight in pointing out everything that was wrong with the world but couldn't care less about real human suffering.

> Hey Supernova, who do you think you are? You are such a snob! You talk big, but you don't care about me and my problems. I'm stuck with the crumbs and you're feasting on some fantastic banquet. You're a hypocrite. You're just like the people and institutions you're always criticizing. Who do you think you are? And what's wrong with me? Why won't you listen to me?

There was no answer. Rana sent her final e-mail with no subject. She hadn't known what to write.

> I'm tired... can you tell what this is all about? What am I doing here, asking all these stupid questions? And what are you doing there, not even listening to me?

Nothing could have surprised her more than suddenly receiving a message the next night.

> From: Supernova.
> I'm here. I've read all your letters. I've answered them by making you ask more questions. I'm waiting for you to ask the only question that matters. Welcome.

19

A Tsunami of the Heart

Eleven o'clock in the morning. The telephone rang. Ferré frowned as he picked up the receiver: "Hello… Yes. Can you call me back later? I'm in a meeting."

"Ferré," Rana said in a soft voice, "I'm in the hospital."

The blood briefly drained from his face. "It's not your heart, is it?" he asked tensely.

"It is, my love," the gentle voice replied sorrowfully. Near her cleavage was a scar from an old operation. Ferré had often touched the mark and told her, "If anything happens to you, let me be the breath in your body." It was hard to accept that he might now have to keep his promise.

"What's wrong? What did the doctor say? Do you have to have an operation?"

"It's my heart. He said that I've fallen in love and it's very serious." He heard Rana giggle.

"Princess, please don't joke," Ferré was utterly confused.

Suddenly a tinge of panic entered her voice. "Ferré, I can't talk to you any more. Arwin wants to take my cellphone. Please pray for me."

The conversation ceased immediately. Ferré was left in the middle of a tsunami of the heart.

FERRÉ

For a long time, Ferré hovered around the hospital entrance. He felt awkward and restless, unable to decide what to do. Never had he felt such agony. Taking his phone out of his pocket, he punched in Rafael's number. Rafael had disconnected his phone. There was no one to talk to.

> *Help me. I can only see her for five minutes and then*
> *only with nine other people. I can't stand the way*
> *they look at me, wondering what I'm doing here. Five*
> *minutes. She looks so helpless lying there. I can't take her*
> *in my arms. All I can do is stand at the end of the bed*
> *and say: 'I hope you'll be better soon' and smile. I want*
> *to be with her all night. But that would look suspicious.*
> *Why do I have to pretend like this? Why can't I stay?*
> *Please help me.*

"Excuse me. You're still here?" someone asked. "Are you waiting for a friend?"

Ferré was startled. It was one of Rana's reporters, eager for a piece of gossip.

"Oh, I'm just about to go. I've been visiting a friend in D-Wing." Even in these circumstances, there was a confidence about his manner. His mask remained firmly in place.

An hour later, two other people passed him and asked the same question.

Three hours later, only the nurses were left. They too looked at him suspiciously. An occasional member of Rana's family looked at him strangely. Perhaps they recognized him as one of Rana's visitors who had, for some strange reason, assumed the role of a security officer.

During the fourth hour, Rana's husband rushed past him. Ferré wasn't sure whether Arwin had noticed him or not. The man looked very tired.

*I don't know you. We have never met. I swear to God
that I don't want to hurt you. I only want what you
already have. It isn't hard to understand why. We are
satellites on parallel orbits, circling around the same
planet. The space is so small, there is only room for one
of us. Please let me have her.*

Ferré couldn't bear it any longer. He called Rafael again. This
time he got through. "Hello? Rafael? I'm at the hospital. Rana is
being operated on tonight. I think I'm going to explode."

"What the hell are you doing there? Go home!"

"How can I?"

"You don't belong there."

"I can't go. It's Rana."

"She has her husband with her. Do I need to remind you of
that? Knock, knock! Hello, Ferré! Go home!"

Ferré wanted to scream. "Please don't joke about this!"

"Me joke? You got yourself into this. You fell in love with the
wrong woman."

Ferré's mouth dropped.

"OK, I'll correct that. Not the wrong person. The conditions
were wrong. You were too late. Whatever! But you can't..."

"Oh, to hell with it!" Ferré angrily snapped his phone shut. The
conditions were indeed wrong but Rafael just didn't know when to
shut up.

In a few minutes, his phone rang. It was Rafael, who proceeded
to try to inject some sense into him. Because Ferré was tired, he said
nothing and let Rafael talk.

"So you'll go home now, right?"

"I'm not sure."

"What else do you think you can do?"

*I'm tired of saying nothing. I want to scream, to shatter
every nook and cranny. I want everyone to hear me
shout out loud: I love her!*

Suddenly Ferré saw the man again. He was standing outside the room, leaning against a wall with a cigarette in his trembling hand. Nervously blowing smoke into the air. There was something pathetic in the way he stood there.

"All right, I'll go home, 'Rafael," Ferré finally decided.

It is at times like this that I need to ask: Where do I belong? Am I as important to you as the ring on your finger? Do I feel as comfortable as your old pair of shoes? Am I as important to you as life itself? Or will you just say my name briefly, then hurry on to other things before you fly back to heaven? Do you understand me, Princess? I want to be here with you.

Ferré cast one last look around the hospital. The building was cold and empty. Ferré felt as though he had been banished.

20

When Thoughts Divide

Diva

The man was in the same corner again. Dark clouds had gathered around him. He was like a boat tossed helplessly about on the heavy seas. His forehead was tightly knit. There was a wild look in his eyes. His jaw was firmly clenched. Despite his torment, he looked wonderful.

And he was writing in a slow, unsteady rhythm, trusting his inner voice. Sometimes inspiration came quickly, sometimes only a few drops flowed.

He had surrendered to the currents. Just as an artist works without asking why he is painting or what is take shape on his canvas.

Diva reached out and touched her window.

I can see how much in love you are, how deeply you drank of that wine. Please give me a few drops for myself. When you finally fall, I want to know how it feels to be strong while the wind howls all around you.

Arwin

Lost in thought, Arwin sat beside his sleeping wife. He could still remember the man's back as he had walked away with such sad heavy steps. Arwin knew how hard it was to draw up anchor when it was time to set sail. It had seemed almost impossible for the man to leave.

Rana had set her heart on that man. It was obvious from the way she looked at Ferré as he stood at the far end of her bed. No one else mattered. He, her husband, was no more than a speck of dust.

> *I promise you this, Rana. As soon as you're better, I'll make you the happiest woman in the world. Perhaps for the first and only time ever. I promise.*

Ferré

> *I'm not a weak man. If I were, I would have run and hidden in a deep valley. I can face the world, I can grasp the truth with both hands, but if you leave me now, I don't know what I'll do.*

Ferré moaned in pain and began to cry. It had been a very long time since he had wept. Some people say that it takes a strong man to be able to cry. But Ferré felt pitifully weak.

A ping-pong ball. That was all he was. Hit from one side of the dilemma to the other, and back again, without anything ever being decided.

Diva

Diva remained where she was. Watching everything. Caught up in the tempest.

> *How far have you fallen, oh man in love? I am waiting at the bottom of the valley. Waiting for you to turn around and discover the real nature of love.*

FERRÉ

Gradually Ferré sensed that he was being watched. He looked up and tried to see who was looking at him.

His eyes settled on a window. Slowly he stood up.

Through the wooden frame, the glass, and the metal blinds, the two people saw each other. As they looked, the space between them vanished. Time took on a new dimension that held its own special meaning.

The world belonged to neither of them. The world had vanished. Only they remained, far far beyond any world.

The Falling Star. As bright as crystal, Ferré heard his heart whisper.

Hello, man in love, Diva called.

DHIMAS AND RUBEN

"Oh, I can't bear it!" Dhimas said, tugging at his hair.

"Pull yourself together," Ruben insisted firmly. "Don't be such a wimp."

"A writer can take sides with his characters, can't he?"

"No shit, Einstein. Even the result of a scientific experiment can be influenced by the scientist's personal tendencies, let alone you, a writer, with your melodramatic instinct."

"In that case, can I...?"

"Remember, we're on a mission. And we can't compromise that mission just because you want to write some fancy story about these characters."

"I wish I could be as businesslike as you are."

"If you were, you wouldn't be a writer. At best, you'd be a mad scientist. If I were as weak as you are, there wouldn't be any intellectual basis to all this romantic carry-on."

"Are you saying that I'm weak?"

"Oh no, not at all," Ruben quickly corrected himself. "You're the most sensitive person I know."

"Thank you for mending your language," Dhimas replied tartly. "Wimp, weak, sensitive: they all mean the same, I assure you. Sensitive sounds classier, that's all."

"But, I'm serious. You are a man of many nuances." Ruben refused to yield on this matter. "Your imagination is as rich in choices as a fractal in the infinite area of a Mandelbrot set."

Dhimas frowned. "What the heck is that?"

"Umm... when a fractal reaches a certain point, it has a multiplicity of choices ahead of it—a whole world of possibilities— as long as it remains untouched by the cortex. Because our thinking is so often dominated by predetermined categories and logical necessities we usually don't even notice these glorious opportunities. The greatest discoveries in the world happen when someone is open to alternative ways of seeing things. Einstein was only five years old when he had the insight into the continuous nature of the universe, which was to become the basis of his theory of relativity. These choices are a very private matter between ourselves and our own private domains. So most people don't appreciate the complex ways other folks think. I certainly don't."

Dhimas shook his head: "What are you talking about?"

"You, you're amazing, Dhimas," Ruben replied. "Without you, my ideas would have no tongue. You are the means by which the nuances in my mind find expression in a way other people can understand. And," Ruben swallowed hard, "I also realize that most people can't stand me. But you can. You have the biggest heart, it can accept my ego and harshness. Dhimas, I apologize for all the cruel things I've ever said to you."

Dhimas listened in silence. There were tears in his eyes. Still, he shouted: "Right! Only a fool like you would preface an apology with all those crazy theories. And only someone who was even crazier than you are would want to spend time with you."

The blood drained from Ruben's face.

"So I must indeed be crazier than you," Dhimas continued softly.

21

The Point of Bifurcation

There was only half an hour. For the first time ever, she had determined Ferré's schedule. Forced him to take time out from the endless hours he devoted to his work. Made him fit the time available to her into his schedule.

They held each other tightly. Ferré's arms made her feel better than any medicine or infusion could have.

"Your being here is the best medicine I could have," she whispered.

Although her loving words inflamed him, he still felt caught in the same paradox.

Yes, Princess, I'm ready to be your medicine. You can chew me, suck me, drink me and swallow me. I'd give up the biggest Strategic Business Development Plan just to be by your side all night. Being with you twenty-four hours a day would be my greatest achievement.

Aren't I strong enough? Determined enough? I'm ready whenever you are. But you're never ready. It is all wishful thinking. None of it is real.

"Rana, I can't go on like this."

Rana had known this moment would come. The crossroads.

"I'm completely powerless when you're sick. There's nothing I can do. That really hurts."

"I understand, I really do." Her eyes shone like brittle glass, ready to shatter at any moment.

"Please don't cry. I don't mean to hurt you. Honestly. But when this happens…" Ferré threw himself into the chair beside her.

"What do you want?" she asked, staring straight at him. *I want you to tell me what you need, so I can be strong enough to give it to you. Please.*

It was the hardest question Ferré had been asked all year. Ironically, he wanted her so passionately that no words could tell her how he felt.

"I want you to leave your husband."

> *No, not that. Too blatant. Or too honest. But certainly not appropriate at this time.*

"I want you to decide for yourself, and stop passing the question back to me all the time, as if it were too hot to hold."

> *Better, but still too direct.*

"Why should love live like some pale shade? Why should it fly through the air like an arrow? I want to put my feet on the ground. I'm tired of always travelling through the sky. I want you for myself."

"I want you for myself."

He had finally said it.

"You want me to leave Arwin. Is that it?"

Ferré was caught in the same paradox again. "It is as if we're still struggling with 'one plus one', when what we need to sort out is one billion five million multiplied by four hundred and thirty-five thousand. You keep asking me what I want, Rana, but you never tell me what it is that you want!"

Rana was startled by the intensity of his response.

"It's a trap. We both know it. You want me to tell you to ask your husband for a divorce. I want you to ask me to take you away somewhere. If we do that, then we can always blame the other one if it doesn't work out. We're scared. We want to be able to say: 'This is all your fault! Look what you got me into.' This is total bullshit, Rana! We're not ready to face reality at all."

Although Ferré's words hurt her deeply, Rana had to admit that he was telling the truth.

"You're right," she said, bowing her head. "We keep going around in circles. We are afraid. And as long as we are, we'll never get anywhere."

Ferré sighed. "I'm not leaving until we settle this one way or the other. We need to make a decision. You decide and I'll accept whatever you decide."

Decide. The word summoned up a multitude of faces, conditions and probabilities. Rana was too tired to think straight. She felt sick in the pit of her stomach.

"I'll come with you, Ferré," she declared unexpectedly, in a firm, clear voice.

Ferré heard a crescendo of violins, as if he were in the midst of a great symphony.

"Rafael?"

"Do you know what time it is?" Rafael was still half asleep and could barely speak. The early dawn call to prayer from a nearby mosque resounded in the background.

"I knew you'd be asleep. But I'm not. I can't sleep."

"So? Why should I be interested? Do you want me to sing you a lullaby over the phone?"

"Sorry, Rafael, but there's something I've wanted to tell you since yesterday afternoon...."

"And that is?" Rafael's eyes were already shutting.

"Rana has finally agreed to talk to her husband. She is going to tell him everything. And she wants to be with me."

"Congratulations."

"That's all?"

"Well, what do you expect? Congratulations. A divorceé, fresh from the oven. What else do you want me to say?"

"I'm serious."

"All right. I know it is what you wanted. But are you ready? What if a hired killer stakes out your house or comes to the office and shoots you? What if her husband gets drunk and comes after you with a machete? What if her family launches a reign of terror against you? Or if someone tells the tabloids and your face appears on Page One as the home-breaker of the millennium? You'll have to be more careful in the future, Ferré, not less. If you think life has been hard recently, don't worry, it's about to get much worse."

"Wow. For someone who has just woken up, your understanding of the situation is pretty good. What trash were you reading before you went to bed last night?"

"Ferré, I want to be sure you're ready. This is going to take a while. All sorts of things can go wrong. Anyway, I'm not a hundred percent sure that Rana was telling the truth. Maybe she just wanted to make you happy."

"That's impossible."

"Don't say 'That's impossible.' I would have said that it was impossible that my good friend, the highly intelligent and rational Ferré, would fall in love with a married woman when he had a thousand other, more feasible, women to choose from. That's a fact, isn't it?" Rafael laughed. "Anything is possible, Ferré."

"I don't care. You can't frighten me."

"Bravo. What a hero. Forward! No retreat!"

"Why do you have to be so cynical?" Ferré demanded angrily.

"I don't mean to be. But you know what I think about the whole business. Even so, I'll pray for the best, whatever that might be."

"Tomorrow is Sunday, isn't it?"

"It is."

"Are you going to church?"

"Probably."

"Please go. And pray for me. Don't forget."

"I'm not sure that God approves of people who play around. Or of divorce."

"I'm not sure that Adam and Eve were married. I think they were living together."

Despite himself, Rafael laughed. "You're crazy, Ferré. But you've got a point there."

Supernova

As soon as the name flashed across the chat room, dozens of other subscribers immediately responded. TNT. Dynamite. Supernova.

Out of the many messages, one was particularly interesting that night.

<guest> Supernova, I'm going crazy.

<TNT> Good. It's about time.

<guest> My whole life, I've only ever loved one woman. My wife.

And I've discovered that she is playing about. For some strange reason, I'm not angry. I don't even feel like blaming her. Do you know why?

<TNT> Why?

<guest> I've seen them together and she looks so happy. She's a completely different person, not the woman I married at all. And I like to see her looking happy.

<TNT> Even though it hurts your feelings?

<guest> It hurts me more to see her when she's with me.

<TNT> How about yourself then? Your marriage? Your rights as her husband?

<guest> I... don't really know. And I don't think I care. Why should I try to hold on to something that doesn't belong to me?

<TNT> Nothing belongs to you. Except your own being. And you are vast. Glorious. You can contain everything, far more than you can ever imagine, once you free yourself from everything else. The more you lose, the more you have.

<guest> Am I crazy if... I let my wife go to another man?

<TNT> It may be the first sane thing you've ever done.

22

Flying Lessons

Day after day Rana woke up covered in a cold sweat. Disturbing scenes played repeatedly in her mind: Arwin running amok; Arwin in a blind rage, totally out of control; her mother weeping hysterically; her parents-in-law fainting; her family and relatives laughing at her.

Like hungry ghosts, these images devoured all her courage, emptied her mind and destroyed her resolution. She couldn't turn to Ferré for support. When they made their decision his strength had meant a lot to her and any display of weakness on her part might destroy both their wills. The stitches in her chest hurt all the time.

Only one hope remained. Anxiously Rana searched for the ICQ number she was convinced would link her with Supernova. Even when she eventually found it, she still knew that there was no way she could be sure that Supernova would respond.

"Come on, where are you?" Rana whispered.

Suddenly she gave a tiny squeal. There it was Online "TNT". That had to be Supernova.

"I know you've come to help me," Rana mumbled. Her weariness and the physical pain vanished, replaced by a clarity of spirit. Like lightning, she typed in her message and sent it off. She kept sending it, until Supernova finally replied.

<guest> Supernova, I want to fly. Teach me how to
block out the noise of the world beneath me. Teach
me how to believe that my wings are strong enough
to carry me. Teach me to believe that I really can
fly.
<TNT> Even birds can fall while they're learning to
fly. Your task is far more difficult because the only
wings you have are your faith in yourself. There is
no other way to learn to have faith in yourself but to
actually have faith.

Rana stopped. She tried to understand the sentences. Did
they mean that she had to abandon all of her rational convictions
and beliefs in order to see the world differently? That she needed
to build up a certain momentum in order to live properly: the
momentum she had when she made her promise to Ferré and had
lost immediately afterwards?

<guest> Do I need to build up a certain
momentum?
<TNT> You can't build up momentum. It is simply
there. And when it's gone, it's gone. It's only a
memory. And a memory won't get you anywhere.
Memories are like rocks at the bottom of a river.
You should flow the way the river flows. Be the river,
not the rock.
<guest> I don't understand: shouldn't we try to
amend our past mistakes? To revive our past
momentum and to try to create a new future? I don't
want to regret what I've done when I'm older. That's
all.
<TNT> You really don't understand, do you?

Rana began to panic. Supernova usually vanished once this
point had been reached.

<guest> Supernova, please don't disconnect. Help me. Explain what you mean.

<TNT> There is a great difference between regretting something and changing it. You can't see that. To regret or to anticipate regret both come from fear. And as long as you're dominated by fear, you'll never get anywhere. Each moment is filled with new and better possibilities. And as long as you're afraid, you'll never be able to realize any of them.

<TNT> You can fly whenever you want to, as long as you believe in the possibility of complete renewal. Enjoy the momentum this belief provides you. For its own sake. Not for anything which the future may bring.

<TNT> You can never predict what will happen in the future. There is only one thing certain in life and that is uncertainty.

<TNT> I can't teach you to fly. You just have to jump and start to fly.

"Rana?"

As if stung by a bee, Rana jumped out of her chair. The bee was Arwin's voice. He reached out and turned off the computer.

"Yes, dear?" Rana asked innocently.

Her husband said nothing. He looked at her in a way he had never looked at her before. His eyes were filled with sorrow, a most profound sorrow. Without his saying a word, Rana could see everything; words could not express the thoughts which passed between them.

They look at each other for a long time. As though they were total strangers.

Carefully the man moved forwards and put his arms around his wife's waist from behind her. He was so silent, so regal.

Rana had never experienced a moment like this. For years they had played guessing games with each other. Now she felt as if she were floating on air. It was a sensation she had never experienced before.

"I know everything."

Arwin's voice was like a glacier, chilling the valleys of her heart.

ARWIN

It was dark. A light rain was falling. His heavy sighs pierced the silence. If one listened hard enough, one could hear the sound of the blood as it pulsed through his arteries.

Slowly tears formed. They assumed their natural place in an unmoving world.

"Please don't cry. I beg you."

The weeping continued.

"If you really love him, I'll let you go. I won't make things hard for you. Or for us. We've both suffered enough. Don't you think so?"

There was no answer.

"I love you, truly love you. You'll never know how much."

The weeping intensified.

"This love that I have for you is great enough to sustain me even without you." He swallowed hard. "It won't be easy, but I don't want to make you suffer any more than you already have. Please," he caught his breath, "please don't cry any more. I've heard you crying to yourself too many times and I can't bear it. It hurts me so very much. I beg you.

"I've tried to deny this for a long time, but I can not do it any longer. You deserve more than I can give you. I'm sorry I'm not the man you want me to be. I was never the husband you dreamed of. But I will always love you, whether you're my wife or not. I will always adore you. And I know that I'll never love anyone else as much as I love you. If only you knew how I felt."

The words carried Rana into a completely different dimension. They helped her to see the face of the man she had married three years ago in a completely new light. The bitterness had vanished. It's often been said that love will set you free. Clearly, Arwin's love was like that, but hers was not and neither was that of her lover.

To Arwin's surprise, Rana toppled from her chair and fell into his arms. It was not a last embrace; on the contrary, it was the embrace of someone who had returned from a long journey.

In her snug little nest, Rana had found the meaning of freedom. She flew at the very moment when she had least expected to.

> \<guest> Supernova, I really didn't expect that to happen. Having struggled so hard to hold on to her, she came back to me at the very moment I let her go. It feels incredible. It feels as though I've been born again.

> \<TNT> You shouldn't try to hold on to anything. You have all you need. Now can you see the futility of struggling to hold on to something? Of trying to possess what you already have? When you let go of your grip on something outside yourself, you move closer to your own integrity.

> \<TNT> To love someone or something with all that you are is the only way to love. If you feel needy or dependent, that only shows how far you are from who you really are.

> \<guest> And I realized for the first time that I not only love her, I love myself as well. I love myself because I love her.

> \<TNT> That is the only Love there is.

Arwin sighed with relief. His face shone with joy. It felt good just to breathe. A new energy poured through his body. He not only had wings: he had become flight itself.

23

Judgment Day

The two men perched in front of the computer. Ruben grumbled softly, "I didn't expect this."

"Neither did I," replied Dhimas, as he wiped his face. He was completely surprised. "It just seemed to happen."

"Are you sure you didn't plan it like that?"

"No." Dhimas shook his head. "I told you: it just happened. I simply put down whatever comes into my head."

"That's strange. The story seems to have a will of its own."

"It is even worse than that. I seem to be part of this story and not just the author. A story within a story. A life within a life. Is that possible?"

"I don't know. There's someone else we need to worry about much more."

"The Knight."

FERRÉ

Judgment Day is a long tongue that licks the bowl clean and leaves nothing behind: no scraps, no crusts on the side of the plate. Judgment Day is a silent explosion that sucks everything into itself, including the remnants of everything it destroys.

Special edition. Read all about it. Your own private Judgment Day.

Rana had vanished a week ago. Ferré could not contact her at all. He knew there was something wrong. Finally the letter arrived. His Judgment Day.

I have no regrets. I hope you don't either. There is no easy way I can tell you this. I'm sure you will understand. I'll never have anything more beautiful than the love we shared (and I hope we will always feel that beauty within ourselves). But I am not the Princess you are looking for. The love we shared has turned into a beautiful diamond and I will keep it forever. Forever. You are very special, Ferré. You have given me the strength to break my own chains. I'm free now. But that doesn't mean we must always walk together. Please allow me to walk on my own path.

Rana

The letter in its plain white envelope was Satan disguised as a spotless lamb. Ferré's first response was blank amazement. His second was to laugh. Laughter seemed a fitting end to the long chain of paradoxes that had assailed him from the beginning of their story. Laughter as a way of expressing his grief and indescribable pain.

Briefly he felt as though he had been caught up in a charade. A stupid tragedy, mixed up with some disgusting soap opera that pretended to be a half-serious work of art. The sort of program that made the tears run down your cheeks, although whether you were laughing or crying was not immediately obvious.

His own cheeks were dry. Not a tear fell. His tear ducts had hardened at the same time as his heart had turned to stone.

Slowly the gray cells in his mind began to work again. What if he hadn't asked her to have lunch with him? What if he'd been busy that morning? What if he'd refused to be interviewed? What if that day had never happened? What if he had never happened?

How would a plate know it was a plate if it were never filled? The Day of Judgment is the beginning of eternal amnesia. And Ferré was a bare plate that could feel nothing but its own emptiness. He was nothing. He hated himself.

The Knight no longer existed. He was dead, together with his love that had dazzled the whole world. He had been turned into a meteor, then into a cloud of fine red dust scattered across the sky. He was finished.

24

Schrödinger's Dark Knight of the Soul

Dhimas could only fold his hands and shake his head. "I don't know what is going to happen next," he said. "Our Knight had recovered the lost fragments of his being. The Poet, the homunculus in him, the subconscious figure whom he once had forgotten about, had come back to him again. He liked himself. But now it has all been taken away from him again. He has lost the lot. Our Knight has been deprived of the greatest thing any human being can have: meaning. If nothing means anything, then life isn't worth living."

"We can't live without meaning," Ruben sighed.

"And what can be meaningful enough to reignite the Knight's life?" Dhimas shouted. "I really don't know!"

Frowning, Ruben tapped his foot against the floor, a sure sign that he was thinking hard. "Do you know what he is?" he asked.

It was obvious to Dhimas he didn't need to answer the question. The bulb had lit up in Ruben's head.

"This is one of the greatest questions in physics today. The dilemma raised by the experiment of Schrödinger's cat. That is what he is: Schrödinger's cat."

"Oh, not now, please," Dhimas said sullenly. "This is a matter of life and death we're working on. Not some magic show."

"I'm not just saying this for show. You have heard of the Schrödinger's paradox, haven't you?"

"Sure. But I can't see how it is relevant."

"It will be, it will be, all I need is some time." Ruben closed his eyes, trying to translate the non-local signals bombarding his brain. "Do you understand what Erwin Schrödinger was trying to do in this experiment?"

Dhimas decided that his best course of action was simply to shake his head.

"He wanted to study the path of a quantum particle, to determine its direction and end point. He designed an experiment with a cat inside a box. The cat is a way of detecting the passage of a quantum particle. The box is rigged with a cyanide capsule and a random triggering device which has a fifty-fifty chance of being activated when a radioactive isotope emits an electron. If the capsule breaks, the cat will die. If it doesn't, the cat will live. After an hour, an observer can open the box and see the result. The question is, what will happen to the cat before the box is opened? Mathematically, the possibilities are that the cat is dead and that it is alive. Both are valid. From the perspective of quantum physics, the cat is half alive and half dead. Until the box is opened, it is in a state of suspended animation."

"Oh, the living dead," Dhimas was beginning to lose patience. "A zombie cat. But what does this have to with our Knight who has locked himself away in his house? How do we know what he is doing?"

Ruben blinked then continued: "Can't you see? He's like Schrödinger's cat. Will he decide to live, will he decide to die, or will he do something else? He has exactly the same chance of leaving his house dead as he has of being alive. This whole thing is like the different ways we can think about an electron!

"You see, quantum physics offers the amazing idea that an electron can exhibit the properties both of particle and wave.

This duality only exists in the quantum domain, where it is called wavicle. It is the observer who decides the outcome. Before the observer intervenes, the electron always has two possible choices. It can be either a wave or a particle."

"You're not making this easy for me," sighed Dhimas. "Let me suggest a different image, something simpler. You and I toss a coin to settle a bet. There are two possible outcomes: heads or tails. The coin could come down either way. But while it is in the air, the coin is half heads and half tails. Is that what you're trying to tell me?"

"Exactly! Why didn't I think of that?"

"So you're saying that our Knight is half alive and half dead? That he has turned into a zombie?"

"According to mathematics, he has."

"That's nonsense. There has to be some other way to solve the paradox."

FERRÉ

For the first time in his life he had spent twenty-four hours alone. He felt so isolated from the rest of the world. None of the outside confusion could touch him. There was only him and it. The nine millimeter pistol someone had given him as a gift. He had never considered using it, until tonight.

On receiving the pistol, Ferré had placed one bullet in the barrel. He had joked about the possibility of playing Russian roulette with it one day. Now he smiled grimly. He had never expected to end his life with a game.

Was his birth into the world nothing more than a game? An example of God's bizarre sense of humor?

Ferré was sorry he had lived such a serious life. Being serious had obviously not gotten him anywhere. But it was too late for all that now.

DHIMAS AND RUBEN

"OK, OK, calm down," said Ruben quickly, as he tried to temper Dhimas' enthusiasm. "There is still Niels Bohr's principle of complementarity. It suggests that the conditions of being half alive and half dead are only abstractions about what might be possible on a transcendental level. It is our observation that collapses one possibility into the other, that turns the dichotomy into a single fact in the same dimension in which we observe what is happening."

"Let me think about *that* for a moment. You're saying that there are now two Knights. In one dimension, he is alive. In the other, he is dead. Is that correct?"

"Well, the principle would seem to divide nature into two parallel dimensions." Ruben was beginning to feel distinctly uneasy.

"But that's great!" Dhimas exploded. "It means that we can write two different stories in two different parallel worlds!"

"Slow down, slow down… it isn't that easy, I mean that complicated," Ruben reassured him. "That would be too difficult. We would need to work twice as hard and deal with twice as much material. It would be very expensive. And parallel universes never interact with each other anyway. From the scientific perspective, it is impossible to set up any experiments which deal with these ideas. They belong more to the realm of science fiction. That's the only place where you find all sorts of crazy examples of completely different dimensions interacting with each other. And you're not writing science fiction, are you? With a dash of scholarly fantasy for added flavor? Are you?"

"No, I suppose not," Dhimas' disappointment was evident.

"Tell me again, what are you writing?"

"A scientific novel, which is romantic, poetic…"

"And real!" Ruben added. "I want to describe real scientific research. And show how those discoveries can be applied to human society."

"Fine. Parallel universes: not important. Please continue."
Dhimas grumbled as he gave in to Ruben. He doused the ideas that
were raging in his mind.

"I'm thinking of a gestalt picture. Do you know what that is?"

"You say such strange things. This is a trap, isn't it? Sometimes
you talk about things everyone knows but in language no one
knows."

"It is your own fault if you don't know." Ruben refused to make
any concessions. "A gestalt picture is one picture hidden inside
another picture. The most famous one is a picture of 'My Wife
and My Mother-in-Law'. They're both present at the same time,
but you can never see them together. You yourself have to decide
whether you're looking at the old lady or the young woman. Each
time you look at a gestalt picture, you have to choose what you're
seeing."

"I know the picture you mean. I just didn't know that it was
called a gestalt picture."

"That's your own loss," Ruben replied defiantly. "Now I can
continue. Reality is like a gestalt picture. We can't tear the picture
into two separate pieces. We can't turn the page over to the other
side. Our consciousness will choose and recognize which choice we
have made. It is the same with the Knight. His consciousness must
choose and determine his future for him."

"I still don't understand. You talk a lot about consciousness. But
what do you mean by the word?" Dhimas was totally confused.

"You have just asked the most important question there is,"
Ruben said firmly. "It's like trying to decide whether Epimenides is
telling the truth when he says that he is lying. If we try to solve this
paradox at the local level, we will be caught up in an endless series
of dichotomies. Material reality. It's non-local."

For a long time, Dhimas was silent. He was trying to relate all
these new ideas to each other.

"Well? Is there still something you don't understand?" Ruben could see the various question marks flying around the room.

"There is, as a matter of fact," Dhimas said in some confusion. "What you were saying about the way in which consciousness can collapse the wavicle aspects of an electron sounded very logical and scholarly. But what would happen if there was an observer and the observer was totally lacking in awareness?"

Ruben smiled contentedly, as though he had already anticipated this question. "It is important here to distinguish between consciousness and awareness. Consciousness is pure, unmediated and takes place in the non-local domain. To collapse one or another of the aspects of the quantum realm, we need awareness. In the psychological literature, consciousness without awareness is referred to as unconscious."

"Now explain to me what you mean by the term 'non-local'. It sounds like a transmission from a UFO."

"Oh, boy, I'm glad you asked that one. It is really very simple. All the signals we receive in the domain of material reality—radio signals, television signals and infrared rays—are local signals. They are bound by space-time coordinates and are limited by the speed of light, while our contact with each other depends on non-local signals."

"But how we can prove that non-local signals exist if we can't detect them?"

Ruben laughed. "You sound just like a skeptical reductionist. Very well, Mr Skeptic, there is an experiment called Faraday's Cage. The cage is a metallic enclosure which blocks out all electromagnetic signals. Any instrument that uses any sort of frequency transmission whatsoever is useless inside Faraday's Cage.

"Two people are put into different cages and the investigators make sure that they can't communicate with each other. But before the subjects are separated, they're allowed to interact for a while, to talk with each other and to build up some sort of psychological bond. Once they've settled in their separate rooms, they are attached to devices that measure their nervous systems, heart rate and other response signals. Do you know what happens? When one subject is asked a question or treated in a certain manner, the other responds in exactly the same way. Even though he is absolutely unaware of what is happening in the next room."

Dhimas was impressed. "That means that we are all interconnected, at a very subtle level, and we're not even aware of it!"

"Often we are totally unaware of what is happening to us. Our bodies receive many million times more stimuli than our brains can handle. Sometimes we're just like corpses. But at other time, we can be fully awake, fully aware, filled with non-local, transcendental consciousness."

FERRÉ

He realized what he had become again: a lifeless robot, without the one chip that gave him any purpose. His obsession with work, the one thing that kept him alive, had been taken from him. He was no longer a workaholic. He was a broken-down robot.

Poet, are you still there? Ferré called over and over again. He wanted one last poem, one last speech before he quit the stage.

After forty-eight hours, there was still no reply. Either the poet had left or was himself dead. There was not even a faint echo. Ferré clenched his fist angrily. *I don't want to die like this.*

DIVA

Diva was suddenly disturbed by what she saw across the road from her house. In an attempt to convince herself that it was true, she looked at her clock again. Half past noon. Why then was the car still in the garage? The curtains were all drawn, including those of the study where the man sat night after night drinking the wine of his love.

Even when the sun began to set in the west, nothing changed. Diva decided not to go out. She had watched the house for five hours and now she felt increasingly concerned. Diva waited for a sign.

The evening gave way to night. The night wore on. Still nothing changed.

When it was time for to sleep, Diva continued watching the house instead. *What has happened to you, oh man who fell so deeply in love? Are you flying high in the sky? Or are you sprawled out at the bottom of some deep ravine of your own making, buried beneath the fragments of your broken heart?*

The next morning, the curtains were still drawn.

DHIMAS AND RUBEN

"We must resolve this paradox," Dhimas worried. "But how?"

"You mean that an observer must intervene," Ruben stared at Dhimas. That was their code.

Dhimas stared back at him. "Our bet. The coin has been tossed, hasn't it?"

Ruben gave a slight nod. Clenching his fist, he said: "I've caught it. Now we have to see which side is up."

25

At the Bottom of the Ravine

Scenes flashed in front of him. In his mind or his heart, he wasn't sure which. And he didn't really care. Both his grandfather and grandmother were there, kneeling in prayer. The rosary beads were beside his pillow, as always. He could hear the drone of the novena, as he did almost every night, his boyish voice reciting the Lord's Prayer. Ferré couldn't understand why he could suddenly witness these fragments from his childhood so clearly.

DHIMAS AND RUBEN

"Why didn't you introduce his past before?" whispered Ruben.

"I have no idea!" Dhimas shrugged. He was obviously as surprised as Ruben was. "Perhaps... there is some other bifurcation he has to deal with. Something other than that story he read as a kid. Something much more serious."

FERRÉ

The fragments continued coming: his grandmother weeping beside his mother's grave; his grandfather holding him tightly the day she died, her body spread out on the carpet. Ferré struggled not to see any more, but the pictures kept attacking him and he could not defend himself. There was a pool of blood near his mother's head, a small pistol in her hand, a letter he couldn't read. Ferré wished the pictures would stop, but now the voices started: "Your mom killed herself," "It was all your dad's fault," "Your dad ran off with another woman." Ferré tried to silence the voices, but now he remembered the comic book, *The Knight, The Princess and the Falling Star*. The sad story of a man destroyed by love. It made him weak then killed him. The same thing happened to his mother and she preferred death to life.

No one ever talked to him about what had happened. There were all sorts of questions he had wanted to ask: Why did they leave me? Didn't I mean anything to them? Were they so busy with their own relationships that they forgot all about me? Why were you so weak and selfish, Mom? Why couldn't you have worked something out, Dad, and not told us? And now... Ferré laughed. Bitterly.

Look down on me from where you are in heaven, Mother, and you, Father, wherever you are. In just twenty-four hours, I've become both of you. I almost ran away with another man's wife, and now, I want to take my own life. Aren't you both proud of me?

Grandma, Grandpa, you always wanted to hear me say my prayers, didn't you? All right. But I won't bow my head or close my eyes.

Ferré looked up, raising his chin as high as he could. Angrily he stared at whatever it was that ruled the universe.

O God, I know we don't talk much but I'm sure You never forget me, just as I've always believed in You. If these are to be my final moments then allow me to speak freely. Accept my reverent complaint. I find it strange

that You show Your glory through those riddles You call
Fate. You make me laugh, even as You mock me.

DHIMAS AND RUBEN

The study was absolutely silent. The two men were completely focused on the screen of their monitor. There was nothing on their mind but the Knight, locked inside his house.

"Despite his exhaustion, he can still fight with the Creator. In a world dominated by conformity, he wants to make God pay special attention to him, and he is prepared to curse God if there is no other way open to him."

"The small gun looked so innocent. Who would have thought that something so tiny can hold the Great Angel of Death who is waiting to steal his soul? His hands are so cold."

Ruben sighed.

DIVA

Suddenly she stood up, opened her curtains, only to discover that the window opposite was still tightly shut. Diva bit her lip. Something important was happening. She could feel it.

You are falling, aren't you? How cold is it at the bottom of the valley of death?

FERRÉ

His hands were as cold as ice. After sixty hours, his blood had almost ceased flowing around his body. Ferré glanced at his reflection in the shining grip of the pistol. He smiled, horrified. *Lord Death, the ruler of the dark and grim Underworld, was extraordinarily attractive.*

DHIMAS AND RUBEN

"He pressed the barrel of the gun deep into his right ear. His finger pressed firmly against the trigger, without the slightest indication of fear."

DIVA

In order to know yourself, you must first destroy yourself.

FERRÉ

Although he was breathing quickly, he was still unruffled. In fact, he seemed distressingly calm. Ferré pressed the barrel against his right temple.

> *Ferré always preferred the right-hand side. He considered the right sphere of the brain to be the most responsible. The left-hand side was the source of cognitive dissidence and needed to be kept under strict control. Or did the two actually work together when all was said and done?*

He moved the target. The pistol was pointed at the middle of his forehead.

> *They say that the third eye is in the middle of the forehead. What a waste that would be. Not that he wanted to see anything once he was dead. He would rather be blind to the whole world. Completely without sight.*

Ferré closed his eyes. That would be a good way to die. But it would have been better never to have been born in the first place.

DHIMAS AND RUBEN

Although it was his turn to write, Dhimas said nothing. He looked at Ruben. Why should he be the one to decide what happened when Ferré pulled the trigger.

"Where is the bullet?" Ruben asked, nervously.

"Ready to be fired," Dhimas replied, swallowing. "The game is at an end."

DIVA

Death to all that you know. Death will free you.

26

Opto, Ergo Sum

Time was almost at an end. And in his last moments, Ferré sensed the complex path time followed. The complexity of the way in which his mind and nerves worked, as his end drew near.

DHIMAS AND RUBEN

The two men looked at each other. Neither wanted to move.

DIVA

Die before you die. Death will free you.

FERRÉ

Something flashed past him, faster than a speeding bullet. It burned through his body like a surge of electricity. And vanished into the distance.

> *Are you the bullet that wounds me, Ferré, and decides*
> *whether my thoughts live or die? I hope that you are.*
> *Let my love flow joyfully and be enthroned in triumph.*
> *My heart is in your hands, it beats at your command.*

DHIMAS AND RUBEN

"Just a moment!" Dhimas exclaimed. "We can't go on like this. It's what is called solipsism—an egotistical philosophy that assumes that the self is the only thing that exists—everyone and everything else exists only in one's own mind. I know it sounds crazy, but I've had this strange feeling again that this story has a life of its own."

Although Ruben did not comment, he too had felt the same thing.

"I don't know what you think, Ruben. But my instincts tell me that he mustn't die."

"No, I don't think he should," Ruben replied, running his hands through his hair. He felt very relieved.

"I have no idea how the story will turn out, even though we're supposed to be writing it. But I do think that we need to use a different approach. I want… a non-local consciousness to speak on our behalf. Whatever that might mean. I want to put the story beyond the grasp of your ego and mine."

"But what do you think is happening to the Knight right now?"

"Let's not think about that for a moment. We need to explore what consciousness is before we can go continue. I really want to know."

Ruben was stunned. He had never seen Dhimas so determined.

DIVA

Rise up from your grave!

FERRÉ

Ferré stood like a statue. His blood flowed fiercely through his body and his flesh stung. Warmth spread through his arteries.

He couldn't believe it. The voice had not come from deep within the labyrinth of his heart. He had clearly heard the words, as though someone was whispering into his ear. And the choices he faced had suddenly vanished. In the twinkling of an eye, an infinite space spread before him and, like Jonah, he had now been cast onto some foreign shore he had never before known.

As he stood on the shore, Ferré wept. Violently. His whole body shook. The tears seemed to rip through his eyes. The voice called his name. The voice was his own.

DHIMAS AND RUBEN

"Right, let's start again," Ruben said, as he returned with his cup of coffee. "There are four different aspects to consciousness. First, consciousness is the field in which the mind processes the world around itself. Second, consciousness is the object of its own awareness of the thoughts and feelings passing through this field. Third, there is the subject: the observer of, or participant in, these thoughts and feelings. And fourth, consciousness is the universal field that contains all of these aspects. David Bohm uses the term "holo-movement" to refer to this fourth aspect: everything is in what he terms universal flux. It is the background against which the whole process of feedback plays itself out. Being universal it simply is, and always will be, even if no activity ever took place. This suggests that, at some deep level, we all share in the one Consciousness. Despite that, we cannot identify with the whole of consciousness, because we are only fragments of it. No one can see the whole picture."

"Now I understand," Dhimas said softly. "Most people identify with their own thoughts. Or with their feelings. And this is what often leads them astray. Thoughts and feelings come and go, they are random, and they change constantly. How can we cling to them?"

"That is what Descartes said: *cogito, ergo sum*, I think, therefore I am," Ruben continued. "And lots of people agree with him."

"You're saying that this really isn't the case?"

"Correct. But I'm also not saying 'I am conscious, therefore I exist.' Such a statement makes no sense. Consciousness simply exists, whether or not we are aware of it, and whether or not we accept that it is."

"But," Dhimas smiled happily, "the important thing we need to learn to say is 'I choose, therefore I exist.'"

"*Opto, ego sum.* I choose, therefore I am."

27

Let Universe Decide

R afael finally heard the news from Ferré's office late one afternoon. Their boss had vanished for three days and no one knew where he was. Multinational corporations were definitely not used to this sort of thing. The wires crackled from one regional office to another. From Hong Kong to New York everyone wondered where Ferré was.

Usually he was available twenty-four hours a day yet seventy-two hours had passed without a word from him. No one could ring him. His home phone had been disconnected at his own request and his cellphone was turned off.

Rafael decided he would go straight to Ferré's house. The Ferré he knew would never stay away from the office without telling someone where he could be contacted. He would certainly never disconnect all his communication devices. That was totally incomprehensible.

Something had happened, Rafael was sure of that. Perhaps his friend had run off with Rana to Las Vegas to get married. Before going on to spend their honeymoon on Maui. Or perhaps they had decided to become Tarzan and Jane in some remote jungle, rather than face all the dangers that would await them in Jakarta.

Across the expanse of lawn, the house looked utterly empty. All the curtains were drawn, no lights were burning. The car sat in the driveway, unwashed.

For five minutes, Rafael rang the bell, pounded on the door and called Ferré's name. There was no response. Ten minutes. As Rafael's suspicions grew, he shouted even more loudly. Servants, bored with their duties in neighboring homes, peered listlessly at him. Stirred by the ruckus, local security guards started to circle.

"Is this where your friend lives?"

Rafael looked around. Diva, Ferré's neighbor from across the road, stood directly behind him.

"Yes. Ferré. Do you know him?"

"Not all that well but I know that he hasn't left his house in three days."

A crowd started to gather.

"Let's break the door down!"

"Can anyone else smell something strange? Maybe he is dead…"

As they chatted idly, Rafael shook his head. Things weren't looking good. Unexpectedly, his phone rang. It was Ferré!

"Rafael, I'm inside," Ferré whispered. "I'll open the door. But get rid of the crowd."

With the stunned look still on his face, Rafael sheepishly set about dispersing the small crowd. He told them that Ferré had just telephoned from out of town. Reluctantly, they slowly drifted away, disappointed that there was to be no show today. Diva remained firmly where she was.

"He is inside, right?"

"Yes," Rafael nodded uncertainly. "But I think you should go too. He said that he won't open the door until everyone goes."

"Don't worry, he won't mind," Diva calmly replied.

Slowly, the handle of the door turned. Through the narrow opening, Ferré saw Rafael… and her!

"Are you all right?" Diva asked at once.

Unfortunately, Ferré was not in a fit state to answer any questions. Despite Rafael's best intentions, Diva immediately took control of the situation. She marched straight into the house, leaving them to gaze awkwardly at each other.

Rafael finally broke through their silence. Staring at his friend, he said: "You look like shit."

Ferré was unshaven and his hair was a mess. There were circles around his eyes. His face was drawn. In the darkness of the house, he looked like a vampire.

"And you smell like it too," Diva added. "Tell your friend to have a shower," she ordered Rafael, "I'll come back with some food."

She turned and walked away, leaving the two men in shock.

"Do you really know her?" Rafael asked in amazement.

Ferré shook his head. He was even more amazed.

Despite his intense curiosity, Rafael did not say a word. There was no need to. Everything was so obvious. It was good that Ferré was sitting peacefully in front of him. Perhaps too peacefully. To be honest, Ferré's tranquility worried Rafael even more.

They sat for a long time, without saying anything.

"Take a vacation," Rafael finally blurted out. "Leave all of this."

"There is nothing to leave."

The silence returned.

"I'm there whenever you need me. But I don't think I can help you very much at the moment." Rafael stood up. "I'm glad you're all right."

"Thank you," Ferré replied sincerely. "I'm glad you came."

Rafael placed his hand on his friend's shoulder. The two men then shook hands, only briefly, but there was something strange about the handshake; there was a strength about Ferré's grip which Rafael had not expected from his recent turmoil. And just as Rafael was about to step out the door, Diva returned bearing a dish of hot macaroni casserole.

"This is all I had. I hope you like it." She showed the dish to Ferré, then looked around. "Would you like some too, Rafael?"

"Uh, no, thank you," Rafael replied as he fled. Too many weird things had already happened on one night.

"I would," Ferré said, despite himself.

"Eat up. You must be hungry."

Later that night, Ferré sat at his dining table, staring at the empty dish in front of him. Life was strange. He had often heard it said that you could never be sure whom you would meet on life's pathway. And tonight he had met a woman who could cook the most delicious macaroni casserole he had ever tasted.

DHIMAS AND RUBEN

"Ruben, before you head back to the kitchen for another cup of coffee, please tell me one more thing."

"Before you criticize my coffee drinking habits again, tell me what you'd like to know."

"I'd like a less scientific explanation of how non-local consciousness works."

Ruben immediately put his cup down and excitedly prepared himself to answer Dhimas. "That's another great question. Do you know why? Because it is the bridge between physics and psychology. I've long been interested in the connections between these two sciences, and with others as well. Communication is a major area in psychology. I want to know about more than inter-personal communication, inter-cultural communication, or even Freud's dark realms of consciousness and the sub-conscious. I want to know how non-local signals transmit their various messages. And do you know something? It is really much less complicated than you might think.

"Non-local consciousness is not limited by the parameters of cause and effect. It works through us. At a certain level, it is us. We usually don't realize that, because a thin veil seems to separate our minds from this consciousness. But the veil is not impenetrable.

Certain mystics and avatars have broken through it from time to time, according to their varying stages of awareness.

"On the other hand, non-local consciousness isn't limited by the continuities of cause and effect. In fact, non-local consciousness depends on creative discontinuities, which emerge moment by moment, situation by situation, as certain aspects of the quantum waves collapse and disappear inside our minds. Creativity relies on quantum leaps and discontinuity. The only way we can communicate is by stepping outside the system."

"Jumping out of the old system."

Ruben nodded, ready to return to the kitchen.

"Just a moment." Dhimas said, restraining him. "If it works through us and if it is just possible that the Knight does actually exist—because I do have a strange feeling that he is outside there somewhere—does that mean that we must ultimately decide whether he lives or dies?"

"Douglas Hofstadter would describe that condition in terms of a 'tangled hierarchy', a situation in which there is no higher or lower level. It isn't really a question of deciding what determines what, the whole plan already exists. Just like the chicken and the egg. As long as you remain *inside* the system, you can go around forever without ever deciding which of the two came first. However, if you are able to step outside the system, it will become obvious that some greater scheme for the species we call 'the hen' already exists. Once you realize that, you can escape the problem. The level outside the system has its own integrity which can never be destroyed. Hofstadter calls it 'the inviolate level.'"

"So, the tangled hierarchy only occurs at the mind level?"

"True. Our perception collapses the quantum realm into a duality and separates the object from the subject. It identifies the self as 'I' and awareness experienced as meaning that 'I exist'. Both of these experiences are part of the tangled hierarchy. At the level of universal consciousness, there is nothing but pure existence."

Dhimas slapped himself on the forehead. "God have mercy on me! I'm so stupid! I said it myself when we tried to stop the Knight killing himself. Solipsism! I forgot that the word 'we' doesn't just refer to the two people in the room. It includes everyone in the whole world. Perhaps there were other people out there who didn't want the Knight to die either... or perhaps he made the decision himself."

"Or, to be more precise, the Universe decided."

Dhimas felt as though he had been sucked up by a hurricane and whirled around with tremendous force. In the kitchen, Ruben whistled as he made himself yet another cup of coffee, completely oblivious to Dhimas' condition.

28

Good Morning, Co-Evolution

"Good morning."

"Good morning. Back to work?"

"Yes. Are you going anywhere today?"

"Not yet. I might go out later in the day."

"Oh! Thanks for the dinner last night."

"You're welcome."

They both smiled. Ferré climbed into his car.

Diva stood where she was, with a trowel in one hand and a bottle of fertilizer in the other. *You have grown wings. Do you know that?*

FERRÉ

Ferré's desk was covered with huge piles of papers. Surprisingly, he wasn't disturbed in the slightest. Even though he had spent half the day explaining his absence, Ferré still felt calm, as if nothing had happened. Even more unusual, he wasn't acting a part or pretending to be someone he wasn't. Ferré felt genuinely good.

He took the rest of the work home. For once, he felt comfortable being alone. His mind was focused and tranquil at the same time. He wasn't daydreaming. He didn't feel stressed.

The study welcomed him like an old friend. It felt warm, natural. There were no painful memories hiding in the corners, ready to attack him. Ferré took the secret letters he had written to Rana and filed them neatly into a drawer. He put the stubby little pencil there, too, thinking at the same time that he should probably throw it away. Then he walked to the window and drew the curtain. As he did so, his hand stopped in midair.

The Falling Star! Standing there, across the way, looking at him. Ferré wondered how long this had been going on.

He raised his hand and waved.

DHIMAS AND RUBEN

They sat comfortably, as if they were in no mood for deep thought.

"Can you see how mysterious life is, Dhimas?"

"Yes. The Knight has decided to write a different story," Dhimas replied, laughing wholeheartedly. "It isn't a simple black-and-white story any more. With a good guy and a bad guy. There isn't any need to decide who is right and who is wrong. Nothing is resolved in anger. It all depends on each person's willingness to reframe the problem."

"That's exactly right!" Ruben exclaimed, as he leaped to his feet. " You are a genius!"

Dhimas was unmoved by the compliment. "Oh, no, I'm not. Ruben, we decided that we'd rest before discussing complicated matters again. Give it up," he sighed. "Let's just keep quiet and enjoy the story."

DIVA

Before long, there was a knock at the door. Diva knew exactly who it was.

"Hi!"

"Hi!" Diva replied. *Obviously he doesn't know that I never receive guests at home.*

"Am I disturbing you?"

"Not in the least. Come in."

"It's strange. We've been neighbors for years but yesterday was the first time we've ever met."

"You're right." *But I did know you. Long before you knew that I knew.*

"And by coincidence we both use the same rooms in our houses as our studies. Forgive me—I didn't mean to spy on you—but did you know we work opposite each other?"

"Then I'll have to ask you to forgive me, too. I didn't mean to spy on you either. By the way, what should I call you?"

"Call me Ferré."

"'Ferré', that's a nice name. I like the way it sounds."

Ferré laughed. "I can't say. I don't usually talk to myself."

"Never?" asked Diva. "Haven't you ever heard yourself call your own name?"

The question flicked like a whip, stinging him fiercely. For a brief moment, Ferré shook as he considered her question. Their eyes locked for what seemed to be an eternity.

Have you ever felt time suddenly vanish, even though the earth continued to spin in its orbit?

I know what you mean. The earth on which you stand keeps revolving. The time in your head suddenly freezes.

Have you ever felt that you are nowhere and everywhere at the same time?

I know that too. It's like you've completely dissolved. It's an incredibly beautiful feeling.

And have you ever spoken, without saying a single word?

Isn't that what we're doing now, Ferré?

Ferré was startled, again.

"I have some special herbal tea. It's my own mixture with three different spices and four flowers. It's nice. Would you like to try some?"

"I really don't want to disturb you…"

"You're not, not at all," Diva quickly replied. "Come in and sit down. I'll make some tea, then we can talk." She disappeared into the kitchen to brew her home-made herbal tea.

They sat on the back terrace, facing the tiny garden and talking like old friends. At times they were serious, at other times they were light-hearted. Sometimes they both frowned. And sometimes they doubled up with laughter.

There was no denying that it was a wonderful night. At least Diva thought so.

"It's dark," Ferré said, glancing at his watch.

"It has been for a while."

"I haven't talked like this with anyone for a long time," he added.

"And I haven't had any visitors for a long time."

"What do you mean?"

"This house has never known visitors, Ferré. You're probably the only other person this tiny garden has ever met."

"I'm honored. Please inform this tiny garden that its mistress considers it the equal of the great Botanical Gardens of Bogor and that she guards it more carefully than any nature reserve in the whole world."

Diva laughed joyfully.

"Shall we meet again in the morning?"

"Outside again?"

"Of course."

Ferré

"Hello? Ferré? Congratulations! I hear you spent the day at the office. Amazing! What are you made of? Cast iron?" Unlike the last occasion when they had met, Rafael now spoke in his normal loud voice. "I tried to telephone you at home but you weren't there."

"Sorry, I went out, and didn't take my cellphone."

"Parading about, no doubt. Where did you go?"

"Across the road."

"To Diva's?"

Ferré could almost hear Rafael's jaw drop.

"You didn't.... Oh no! Hey, dude, you did use protection, didn't you?"

"Don't be such an idiot! You don't think I slept with her?"

"Well, excuse me! A guy with a broken heart suddenly realizes that he has a beautiful neighbor who is very available: as long as he has the money, which he does. It would seem a reasonable assumption."

"Don't talk about Diva like that. She isn't like that at all. We just talked, for hours."

"You just talked? For hours?"

"It's incredible how much she knows. We talked about the free market, the internet business, third world debt, labor issues. We even discussed Marxism."

"Eat my shit!"

"And she can quote extensive figures and statistics, not only for one or two countries, or a couple of big corporations, but for lots of them. It's as if she's worked for many companies or had hundreds of researchers supplying her with information."

"Maybe she is really a spy and not the working girl she seems to be."

"Just keep your ideas to yourself."

"OK, OK, at least I'm pleased to hear that tone in your voice again."

"Which tone?"

"You never realize, do you! God knows what would happen to you if I wasn't here." Rafael chuckled. "That tone. The sound you start to get in your voice when you're attracted to someone."

"You really think you know everything."

"Maybe we've never talked about Karl Marx, maybe I only know about spare parts and that sort of crap, but in this regard I'm never wrong. The facts speak for themselves."

"Believe whatever you want, my friend."

"But I salute you. Your tastes are absolutely consistent. Nothing but the very best is good enough. First it was," Rafael swallowed hard, "someone else's wife." Then he lowered his voice slightly. "And now…" Rafael could not continue. Instead, he lapsed into silence.

Ferré couldn't help himself. He laughed.

Rafael resumed his questioning, and soon they were both laughing, until they were both doubled over, with tears running down their cheeks.

DHIMAS AND RUBEN

"This is wonderful," Dhimas said with warmth. "The Knight and the Falling Star have started to become good friends."

Ruben looked at him resentfully. "Don't get too emotional. There are some things I still need to explain."

"That's right, go ahead and sulk. You're ruining the mood, do you realize that?" Dhimas was annoyed. "What is this latest headache you have for me?"

"It's a concept explaining how reality can change so drastically: co-evolution." Ruben's excitement was obvious. "Co-evolution is a real break-through in biology, a completely new way of thinking about Darwin's ideas. Increasing evidence shows that the struggle for survival of each particular species depends not on its competing with every other species, but on its willingness to work together with them in the same ecosystem. Those who survive learn to cooperate. What is happening in your story is more or less the same as what happened on the earth two billion years ago."

"Only two billion years ago? Are you sure it wasn't longer?"

"At that time, the surface of the planet was covered with bacteria. Nothing else existed. One type of bacteria, now called *cyanobacteria*, produced oxygen, which was actually a poisonous gas in those days. When the biosphere reached a critical state, there was widespread destruction. As a result, the surviving bacteria had to find new ways in which they could work together. Some of them went underground in order to avoid the gas. Others developed the ability to breathe oxygen.

"The two types combined and produced a different sort of bacteria, one with its own nucleus. And that bacteria mutated into an oxygen-using bacteria, which successfully invaded other bacteria and eventually produced mitochondria, which to this very day forms part of the cells in our body. Still other host bacteria were invaded by cyan, and they learned how to produce chloroplasm from sunlight and water. Scientists suspect that this was how the first plants began."

"That is remarkable. But I can't see what it has to do our story."

"Nothing yet. But the microbiologist Lynn Margulis has some interesting ideas to add to this. She has argued that the hybrid created by a host bacteria and the highly mobile spirochetes bacteria represent the first step toward the eventual formation of the brain. When you think about it, the whole thing is pretty ironic. Spirochetes move extremely quickly, yet the poor things were imprisoned inside the human skull. So they lost their identity as spirochetes and instead took on a new form and a different function: they turned into brain cells. Despite their containment in an extraordinarily tight space, they became the means for the fastest system of feedback known on planet earth: the human mind. Having escaped from their place in primitive mud they assist today in the rapid electronic process known as thought."

"Ruben, I'm sure you're right. The sexual relations of bacteria are fascinating. But I still can't see what this has to do with our story."

"This is what co-evolution is all about: the ability of living creatures to change their environment, to turn enemies into friends, and to create new life. Believe me, this doesn't just happen at a physiological level. It is also a mental process. If even primitive bacteria can change the context in which they live, it staggers me that human beings can't find anything better to do than simply surrendering to whatever comes along. Every level of existence bears this possibility, from a single-cell bacterium through to us!"

DIVA

"Hello, good morning!"

"Good morning!"

"How's your pepper plant doing?"

"It has started to blossom."

"Congratulations. You'll soon be a mother."

Diva gave a soft chuckle.

"Are you staying home today?"

"Hmm, probably. I thought I might bake some cakes. If I do, would you like to try some?"

"Sure."

"I'll see you later then."

"I'll see you later."

As she stood watching the car disappear into the distance, Diva raised a hand and pressed it against her breast. She could feel the warmth streaming through her body. It was real. *Is this how you used to feel, when you were drunk with love?*

FERRÉ

He looked at the cupcake in his hand. The fragrant aroma of pandanus palm rose from the tiny holes in its surface. The mixture must have been perfect, he thought to himself, with just the right amount of baking powder. He could hardly wait to taste it. The cake would melt in his mouth.

"Are you conducting a chemical analysis, Ferré?"

"More or less." He laughed. "I've felt so strange these last few days. I seem to be interested in the tiniest things. Once I wouldn't have noticed them at all. Now I do, and I can't help staring at them in wonder. That is so strange, isn't it?"

Diva smiled and sipped her tea.

"The rupiah has fallen again today."

"Two hundred points, right?"

"Yes. It's much worse than the baht or other Asian currencies."

"But for the same reason. No local confidence in the currency. People are bored by the whole situation."

"Everyone wants the president to stop making statements which are not conducive to a recovery."

"In my opinion, the whole country is turning into a museum."

"A museum?"

"We're out of date. Look at what is happening overseas," Diva continued. "Financiers rule the world. They have far more attractive and dynamic markets than Southeast Asia to play with. They can buy and sell whatever they please, including each other." She shrugged, then continued: "Tell me, Ferré, what sort of god rules the world of big business?"

"Money, of course. And the stockbrokers are his prophets."

"If we can trace the evolution of any one object in this world from its very beginning, that object would have to be money."

"I agree. The evolution of the concept of money is amazing."

"Capitalism is the most comfortable breeding ground imaginable. Of all the many economic systems, money chose capitalism as the most enduring, and the most capable of surviving historical changes; a true survival of the fittest; and it has mutated within capitalism in ever more sophisticated ways to become increasingly immune to attack, increasingly intelligent. If you think about it, money has taken on many divine qualities. Even the greatest fiscal atheist can't live entirely free of material constraints. You can't avoid money. It provides the context in which our lives are lived. And it takes so many shapes and forms: paper, coins, shares, land, the forest…"

"…Our bodies, minds, images and ambitions. Money is absolutely universal. Like music… or mathematics!" Ferré looked at Diva in awe. "I've never thought about money in this way before. It's fascinating."

"And we teach other new lessons about money every day," Diva continued. "We even teach those lessons to our children. As soon as someone knows about money, he transforms into a taxi and can't go anywhere without his meter running! He starts to count, calculate and measure the worth of everything he sees."

"Everything except for one thing," Ferré interrupted her.

And during that brief interjection, a few seconds at the most, they looked directly at each other.

You know precisely what that one thing is.

I do. It is in you.

And in you.

It cannot be calculated.

It can only be felt. And it feels so warm, doesn't it?

Warm? I could burn up the whole earth, Ferré.

"Another cupcake?"

"Yes, please."

After he had returned home, Ferré searched for something in one of his desk drawers. Rana's letter. He read it several times, then carefully folded it up and put it away.

You were right, Princess. The love we shared has turned into a beautiful diamond and I, too, will keep it forever. Forever.

Dhimas and Ruben

Dhimas could just hear Ruben lecturing him from the kitchen: "At the point of bifurcation, everything crystallizes. You can never return to that moment, but it will stay with you forever."

For a moment Dhimas stopped typing, annoyed that what he was writing was exactly what Ruben was saying. Yet again he wondered why he seemed to be the victim of so many coincidences. Or, better put, so many *miracles.*

29

Have You Ever, Supernova?

"Good morning" and "I'll see you later" became the sentences they most wanted to hear. Sometimes they bade "Sleep well" to each other from a distance, with a wave of a hand before they drew their curtains. They never went out together. Instead, they sat in Diva's little garden with a pot of tea and two cups and sometimes a plate of cakes. And they talked, all the time. Only two topics were never discussed: why Ferré had locked himself away in his own house and Diva's occupation.

Rafael was flabbergasted. "I don't understand it. You're together almost every night. So when does she work? In the middle of the day? SAL: sex after lunch?"

"I don't know and I don't want to know. It is clear that she has given up modeling. When I ask her in the morning, she usually tells me that she isn't going anywhere that day."

"And you believe her? Ferré, please! You are so naïve!"

"Why should I think she was lying to me? What would be the point of that?"

"Sure, sure." Rafael nodded with conviction. "You'd rather not know, because if you did, you'd only be hurt. And you don't want to be hurt again."

"She is the most independent person I know. And she is old enough to know what she wants to do with her life. So why should

I worry? And if you think I'm jealous, in a coarse and vulgar way, then you're absolutely wrong. We're just good friends. Nothing more than that."

"But she is special, isn't she?"

"Very much so. I won't deny that."

"Then what are you waiting for?"

"For Pete's sake, stop thinking in clichés. You'll make me sick."

Rafael giggled. "Hey, I was only testing you. And you're worse that I thought. You don't want to be an item, but I know how you feel even if you don't: and it is worse than either of us can imagine."

Ferré was startled. Rafael may have had the prophetic insight of Nostradamus as far as his own love life was concerned, but Ferré hadn't realized before that he was quite so easy to read.

SUPERNOVA

The modem merrily clicked like a choir of crickets. A shining pair of eyes waited for the word "connected" to appear. Almost immediately, the messages began to arrive. After quickly sorting through them, the hands moved to the *reply* button.

The work was all consuming. Intellectually demanding. Physically punishing, as fingers danced across the keyboard.

>Supernova, do you believe that our destinies are
decided before we're even born?

I believe in a process of mutual decision making.
Fate is an interactive process. It just doesn't flow
in the one direction. Whatever you do or think has
consequences for the rest of the world, whether
you know it or not. It is the same for the Earth. The
planet is alive too. If we were sensitive enough,
we would see that we're engaged in a constant
dialogue.

It is like two pen pals living in the same body.

>Do you believe in Heaven? Hell? In angels? Or
demons?

I believe that we each create our own heaven,
our own hell, that we can behave like angels, and
demons as well.

<send>

>Supernova, do you believe in God?

Believe? I see Him everywhere. Each moment.
Even between each moment. But I don't think you
and I share the same understanding of God.

<send>

>I'm curious about just one thing... have you ever
been in love?

The nimble hands came to a complete stop. This was not the first time the question had been asked. A foolish question, from some confused person, completely unknown to Supernova. But now there was no simple answer. Had Supernova ever been in love?

In response, the hands moved to shut down the computer.

Gio

"*Aloa*, Gio?"

"*Aloa, querida!* This is a surprise!"

"What time is it there? I hope I'm not disturbing you."

"Four o'clock in the afternoon. Siesta time. But you know me. I can't sleep during the day."

"Gio, I want to tell you something."

"Is everything all right?"

"I'm ready to go."

There was a long silence.

"Gio…"

"Are you serious, Diva?"

"I need some information from you."

"Are you sure about this?" he asked earnestly.

"Hey, I'm an eccentric millionaire with more money than she knows what to do with," Diva joked. "Of course I'm serious."

"I'll come with you. Anywhere you want to go."

"*Nao, querido.* I'm going by myself."

Gio sighed. "Fine."

"I'll send you an e-mail tonight. Please read it. OK?"

"*Sim,* will do!"

"*Muito obrigado,* Gio."

DHIMAS AND RUBEN

"It is time to finish the story, Ruben."

"How?"

"I don't know. Do you have any suggestions?"

Frowning, Ruben swung his feet back and forth under his chair while he waited for the light bulb to switch on.

"Aha!" The shout came from Dhimas.

"I hope the idea is as exciting as your voice suggests."

"Yes!" Dhimas' eyes bulged. "We'll let the story finish itself!"

Ruben's eyes popped. "Wow! What a brilliant idea! Where did you get it from? The loony bin?"

"I knew you would love my idea. Look, we have reached the climax of our story. It is time to see whether we believe what we preach. That's the point of—what's that term again?—bifurcation?"

"Are you mocking me?"

"We've both felt that this story has a life of its own. The number of coincidences has been astonishing. Hasn't it ever occurred to you that we too might be part of this tangled hierarchy? The key to resolving the whole thing could be anywhere. It doesn't matter any more. The important thing is the grand plan. On the inviolate level, like you said. So, what if we just put down our pens and let the story unfold, all by itself? Sooner or later, we will reach the end. One way or another."

Ruben's face clearly betrayed his inner conflict.

"Don't you want to join in the game and make a quantum leap the same way they are?" Dhimas smiled broadly. "First we need to turn things around, Ruben. Look into the mirror. Stop manipulating the plot and become part of it ourselves."

Ruben shook his head. "It's crazy, but I can see what you're saying. But how do we do it? Is it really practical?"

"Be quiet," Dhimas firmly replied. "We both have to be quiet. And let the true storyteller reveal himself."

"What sort of quiet? Not ask any more philosophical questions? Stop thinking? Or sit still and not even touch our work?"

"All of that."

30

Through the Looking Glass

It was about one-thirty in the morning. The words in the book began to blur. He could no longer fight off sleep. His eyes closed. Disjointed thoughts passed through his mind. Then it was dark. And absolutely silent.

Gradually, he could hear the sound of someone weeping into a pillow. A girl, crying. Heavy steps echoed down a corridor, a door softly squeaked open. A voice whispered to her, telling her that she was different from the other children and that she was very beautiful. Ferré felt cold, as though he were being stripped of his clothes, one piece after another. The child moaned, as a terrible pain forced its way through her crotch. Over and over again. The pain never stopped. For years. The weeping became more pathetic. There was anger, endless disappointment, and demons everywhere dressed in white robes. The demons taught the children how to pray. They preached the greatness of God. They quoted the Scriptures.

God seemed to be stuck somewhere else, unable to help. Almost every night she reached out to Him for help and He never heard her pleas. Demons, angels, people and pictures were all jumbled together in her ever-growing confusion and anger. The pain was unbearable. And then finally the child exploded.

Each cell in her body shattered and a vast electrical current surged through every part of her. Everything suddenly went black. Pitch black. But somehow she wasn't afraid. On the contrary, she felt very peaceful. She was peace itself and no longer imprisoned in her body. Was she dead? It seemed like it. She no longer existed yet she was everywhere. There was nothing more she needed to ask. There were no limits and no material barriers. The only thing that remained was eternity itself.

Trillions of sparks appeared, turning the darkness into light. The light was as pure as a drop of dew on the first day in the Garden of Eden. The world assumed its original purity and she saw herself everywhere. The air was filled with color. Fragrances tickled her nose. She felt the whole Sahara in one tiny grain of sand on her arm.

The bruises on her flesh vanished. There was no more pain. Her skin became fine and delicate. Her eyes shone brightly and each nerve in her body was incredibly sensitive. A slight protrusion formed in the middle of her forehead.

Each moment was new, unique. If she ate one apple, it felt as though she had consumed a whole basket of fruit. Her mind was free of old memories. She only thought when she wanted to. Knowledge was there for the taking. She could understand any book as long as she set her mind to it.

Later, when her feet were on firm ground again, her wings remained. She could let go of her body at will. Her only wish was to enjoy life. To play. Pleasure and pain, tears and laughter were all the same to her. She could experience these different emotions, and respond to them, but she was not bound by them.

She became a mirror of everyone around her. If someone hated her, that person really hated himself. If she made love with someone, that person was making love to himself. She was simply a channel for energy to pass through. And when she fell in love.... Ferré's attention was suddenly distracted.

He saw a mirror nearby and, walking over to it, he slowly stretched out his hand and touched it. The glass rippled, like the surface of a pond. When the waves settled, the image in the mirror gradually changed. Ferré fell to his knees. The image in the mirror... was Diva! His soul shook. His heart was torn to shreds. His brain seethed. His body exploded.

Ferré sat straight up. He was breathing heavily and his whole body was covered in a cold sweat. *Was I dreaming? I don't know. It all seemed so real: the pain, the explosion, the innocence of Eden, the mirror, Diva!*

Like lightning, Ferré leaped to his feet and ran to the door.

Diva had left her door ajar. Ferré hesitated, then decided to go in. Inside there was another door, which was also open, the door to Diva's study. In front of the computer was a large chair with its back to the door.

The chair spun around and Diva greeted him with a smile.

"Ferré. I've been expecting you."

DHIMAS AND RUBEN

"To be honest," Ruben said with a sigh, "I can't bear this any longer."

"What can't you bear?"

"I can't bear being quiet!"

Dhimas giggled. "I knew that theory would get the better of you," he said.

Ruben began to pace around the room. "Don't occasions like this make you want to doubt the concept of free will? On the one hand, God is supposed to have made us autonomous creatures. On the other, everything has already been decided for us, predetermined: it is our fate, our destiny, and all we can do is accept it, just as we are doing now. Be quiet, surrender and wait for a miracle to fall from the skies."

"Hey, hey, take it easy. Why have you suddenly become such a pessimist?"

"I just want to talk about it," Ruben said in his own defense. "This is exactly the same paradox Wigner found himself in when he tried to resolve Schrödinger's paradox."

"I'm not sure I want to hear this," Dhimas pleaded. "Paradoxes giving birth to more paradoxes."

"Eugene Paul Wigner suggested the idea of multiple observers, more than one of them. And that provides a paradox in itself. Which of the observers do we credit with collapsing the wave aspect of an electron? So what if Wigner was right? The observers come to the same decision because they have experienced the same sensations in response to an identical situation. So why should we worry about free will, if all sensations produce the same response? What's the big deal? The concept is ridiculous."

Dhimas listened patiently to Ruben's argument, without being upset in the slightest. "Ruben, if your idea of free will is nothing more than the rebellious demands of a small boy for ice cream when he has the flu, then it is indeed nonsense. The universe wouldn't give us such a trivial attribute. I believe that free will is the human ability to adopt new perspectives. If you lost all your money tomorrow, would that be a disaster or a hidden blessing? It is all up to you. Free will is the will to recontextualize situations. As my friend just said… Uh, what was his name again, Ruben?"

Ruben clicked his tongue, half with anger, half in amusement. "Now I'm the one who feels stupid! I'm like a cat chasing its own tail."

"Perhaps that is what life is like in a world of duality. No matter how much we know, we are still no more than thin blades of grass bending in the wind. Unstable and easily upset. We're still human, Ruben."

DIVA AND FERRÉ

"Who are you really?" Ferré asked, fascinated.

"I'm your last lesson before you fly. It began with the fluttering wings of a small white butterfly and ended with a bright falling star. You have undergone a most wonderful and mysterious transformation, Ferré."

"You haven't answered my question," Ferré said angrily. "Who are you? And who sent you? How could you enter my dreams? Was it a dream, or..."

"You have so many questions, and none of them are necessary." Diva laughed. "I am an ordinary human being, just as you are. We are all mirrors for each other. But my mirror is clean. I see myself in you, in other people, and in the world around me. I am reflected every moment, and I gaze in awe at one beautiful sight after another. Am I dreaming? It doesn't matter. Why should it? Lots of people have their physical eyes open but are spiritually asleep. What truly matters are the eyes of the soul. And your eyes are open now.

"Ferré, you sent for me. You created everything that has happened to you. It was your own desire that brought all this about. And look! Now you truly are a Knight. You fell, but you rose again. You crashed to earth, but you were not destroyed."

Diva slowly arose from her chair and approached him. She gently caressed his cheek. Her hand felt warm, comforting. Ferré closed his eyes. Diva caressed his very heart.

There have been times when I have tried to destroy my own soul...
Let me take the bullet for you.
There have been times when I have felt nothing.
Let me feel for you.
From the moment I began to fall through the air...
I let you go so that you could be absolutely free.

I love you, more than you will ever know.
     You love who you are, more than you will ever
     know.

"So, what comes next?" whispered Ferré, holding Diva's hand tightly.

"I'm leaving."

Ferré sighed. His jaw tightened. *I thought so.*

"The world is a vast playground, Ferré. I want to travel. I want to play. But I also need your help."

"Just tell me what you want."

"I want to set up a private educational foundation, without using my own name. There is enough money to establish a school and to pay for various projects. The school will be for everyone, with no limits on the age. It will teach only one thing: How to understand life. It will ask only one fundamental question: 'Why?' not 'What?' as other schools have always done. It will not be confined to a set of buildings but freely available on the Web. I need a small, professional team to manage it efficiently and you are the only professional person I can trust."

"And what about you?"

"No desk can hold me, you know that. My office is the entire virtual world. I'll sell everything in this house except for my notebook. It is the only networking tool I need." Diva smiled. "The network can evolve in any direction it decides. We can help it grow. Ultimately we must all share what we have learned in our own lives. We can watch the silver threads endlessly reach out and join as they see best."

Like the sun at dawn, a smile slowly spread across Ferré's face. "It will be an honor, Supernova."

Diva looked surprised.

"I have visited a particular kindergarten many times and often wondered who Supernova really was. Then I met you and I hoped that Supernova might turn into Diva. Then, one day, I asked a certain question, and there was no reply." Ferré placed his cheek next to Diva's face and whispered into her ear: "Have you ever been in love, Supernova?"

And in response, Supernova whispered: "I see myself in love when I look through your mirror, my Knight."

31

The Web

Ruben snored softly on the couch. Dhimas, however, was wide awake as he stared at each sentence that appeared on the screen of his computer.

"This is crazy," he whispered to himself. Over and over again his hand clicked at the mouse, as he continuously struggled to work out who was sending the messages, to what organization they belonged, and how their e-mail address had come to be added to the list of recipients.

This is a KINDERGARTEN.

Your opportunity to play with life. To really LIVE.

This classroom provides you with information. It is not a chat room.

For all our sakes, I want to avoid useless details that will only lead to stupid arguments.

If you have any questions, send them to me, Supernova,

and I'll answer you directly.

Dhimas couldn't wait to wake up Ruben.

DIVA

"Gio, I've decided the first place I want to visit."

"Where?"

"The Apurimac River."

"Wow! Straight to the Zeus of all rivers. What an extraordinary choice."

"I want to ride the rapids, Gio. There are a lot of rivers to experience."

"Make sure you visit Machuu Pichuu. I have a friend there, Paullo. I'll let him know you're coming."

"*Obrigado.*"

"After Apurimac?"

Diva paused for a moment. "Tatshenshini."

On the other side of the world, Gino smiled.

"Do you have any special tips for me, *querido*?"

She heard him sigh.

"Yes. Watch out for the grizzly bears."

It was Diva's turn to smile. "You're very special. I hope you know that."

"Don't expect me to tell you that you're special, too. You're... you're the sun that shines in my life, Diva."

DHIMAS AND RUBEN

Their heads exploded with one surprise after another, like fire-crackers thrown onto a bonfire. The e-mails shocked them more than the storm of serotonin had ten years ago.

Their fiction had turned into reality. It was far more than rows of black letters on a white screen; their lives had been caught up in the spiderweb they had created inside their own minds.

SUPERNOVA

– For those who want to LIVE –

Welcome.

Today Supernova wants to invite you to the movies.

Do you remember the last time you watched a film you really enjoyed? From the start, the screen was full of light and color. You were moved. The film made you cry, made you laugh, perhaps even made you ready to kill someone.

At that time, you were an observer. A passive observer, reacting to active virtual stimuli. What was the purpose of those stimuli? They only had one goal: to reproduce themselves through you. You think those stimuli are not alive but they are. Very much so. They are like a virus, beyond simple definitions of life and death, searching for the right host. Whether you respond positively or negatively doesn't matter. They come alive the moment you begin to react. You give them meaning.

Now let's take a different position.

You are one of the figures on the silver screen. The script, the whole plot, is deeply woven into every cell of your body. Your body is mature, ready for love and sexual intimacy. Ready to reproduce itself. Ready, without your even knowing it, to create more hosts in which the viruses can continue to live.

Can you see the basic similarity between these two positions? That's right. In both cases, you are being exploited. Scientists have long known about the stimulus which drives your body to reproduce itself, the same way the marmot does; they call it DNA. If, in your egotistical way, you think that you are more important than DNA, simply because you can see your body but you can't see DNA, then I suggest that you think again. You are an empty space in which DNA has created their kingdom.

Does that make you feel small and worthless? Then relax. There's still more to come.

It is more abstract, too. The stimuli send their fine, hidden signals into the superb recording and playback machine which is your brain. When you think you've discovered an idea, the idea has really discovered you. When you think you have an idea, the idea has you.

For almost three decades, scholars have been talking about memetics. This science studies memes, the basic building blocks of thought, which provide the foundations of culture, society, belief systems, and everything connected with the way in which we interpret life.

If, in your distress, you want to get rid of memes, I have some bad news for you. No microscope can detect them. The only instrument you can use to study their spread—and this is the good news—is your own understanding.

Allow me to give you some simple advice. If you dissect DNA molecules, you will eventually discover that they are empty. If you dissect words, you'll find that they consist of meaningless letters.

All these empty forms contain their own story. And most of us can only feel the residue of those stories, the conflict contained in them. In our lack of consciousness, we feel like targets.

Now allow me to give you some additional advice. First: Accept the fact that everything is relative. Day by day, science, theology, and philosophy all show that we live in a world where everything is relative. This truth is relative. What you read here is relative.

Conflict can only cease when you reach point zero. Then you will see the various forms of self-defense you have erected around yourself, but you will no longer be subject to them. Life will stop being difficult and, instead, turn into pleasure garden.

I would like to show you how to see everything from two different perspectives: that of the director and that of the actor. Once you become conscious of the need to overcome this duality, you will be able to move from one perspective to the other at will in order to accomplish whatever you want in life.

That's right. Whatever you want.

Are you ready?

If you'd rather remain enslaved to DNA, to be harvested the way your friends the marmots are, then please close down your computer. If you're happy to rent yourself out to various memes, so that they can use you as a means of storing and processing data, let me know and I'll take you off my list of subscribers. But if you agree that life is full of obscure mysteries waiting, indeed eager, to be explored, then come join me on this journey.

It will not be an easy journey, but it will be you journeying in search of YOURSELF. Get out of your grave.

"Memetics," Ruben hissed in amazement. "The wench knows about memetics."

"What should we do?" Dhimas nervously whispered.

"Coffee. We need coffee."

"Make one for me as well."

SUPERNOVA

The slender fingers typed as fast as lightning. There were too many e-mails to answer, almost too many questions flooding from the ICQ chat room. Suddenly a new address appeared on the screen. Supernova smiled. The first line said everything.

<guest> Cyber avatar. So you do exist.

<TNT> I'm pleased to meet you both.

<guest> How do you know there are two of us?

<TNT> I know all those whom I have chosen.

<guest> You've chosen us?

<TNT> This network is too vast for me to handle by myself. I need other people to help me.

<guest> Do you mean... us?

<TNT> There aren't many other people I can trust.

<guest> But why us?

<TNT> Because most people aren't interested in paradigms of wholeness. I'll get back to you.

As soon as she closed the chat room, another message flashed across the screen. She was delighted.

<guest> Open your window, Supernova.

Laughing, she drew back her curtain. Ferré was at his window and waved to her.

<guest> I always look forward to this moment.

<TNT> So do I.

<guest> I love you.

<TNT> I do too. More than you will ever know.

32

Individuality is an Illusion

Time is greedy and never satisfied. It swallows far more seconds than it has on its plate. Stole the hours he should have been spending holding Supernova in the days to come.

"Don't let it consume you, Ferré."

Ferré was startled. It was difficult being with someone who knew everything he was thinking.

"Hush," Diva whispered before he could say anything. "Listen..."

The heart beating. The breath sighing. In silent harmony.
The rhythm of a poem that has no end: Life.
And when the heart stops beating?
The poem is the spirit wrapped in words. The spirit never dies.
Never?
It is everything. Where can it go? You already have everything.

"Will we ever meet again?"

"Of course. I don't know when or where in this world. I might be Diva the cake seller when you meet me next..."

"Or Diva the gardener."

"A fine profession." Diva laughed.

"Don't forget to bring a pot of tea and some freshly baked cakes."

"I'll be waiting for that moment, Ferré."

Ferré slowly put his arms around her. He could feel warmth spread as he touched her. A warmth that joined their two bodies together. The shape of her body beneath his hands. He drowned in the spaces between her ribs, her shoulder blades. He was lost among the fine hairs on her neck. He allowed his breath to slowly sink into every pore of her flesh.

The blood pounding. Energy dancing.

The elemental harmony of love.

DHIMAS AND RUBEN

"Explain it to me, Ruben! I don't care how complicated it is. I just want an explanation!" Dhimas was almost beside himself in his confusion.

Despite this, Ruben lay back comfortably and stared at the ceiling, a smile covering his face. "Relax, Dhimas. This was all your brilliant idea. Enjoy it."

"I know! But it's too good to be true!"

"Autopoiesis. That's all I need to say."

"Thank you. That tells me a lot," Dhimas said angrily. "Excuse me, but can you explain the difference between autopoiesis and Caspar the Clown?"

Ruben laughed. "Oops, sorry. All right. If we spread out the different systems in the world along a continuum from the most simple to the most complex, then autopoiesis would be at the very far end. It is so complicated that autopoietic creatures are a complete paradox. Structurally each creature has the capacity to reproduce itself. Each of their organs is highly autonomous. Even when taken into more complex networks, they still retain their individual identity. But on the other hand, because autopoiesis is such an open system, the same creatures are also completely dependent on their environment. However, the environment itself is never stable. There are always severe fluctuations in the amount of energy available in the form of food, sunlight, chemical elements, minerals and so on. Thus, every autopoietic structure has its own unique history. This history is, nevertheless, interconnected with the wider history of every other autopoietic structure, and so on and so forth. The more autonomous a creature is, the more it depends on everything else. There is really no end to it."

"Which means?" Dhimas impatiently interrupted.

"Individuality is an illusion."

Dhimas was stunned. Gradually, he was beginning to see the various connections with increasing clarity.

"Reality is true. Our separation from it is not. At one point in time, we are all one vast organism. Spirit and matter come from the same source. They are two aspects and one as well. And those events which seem to cross over between the two are not as mysterious as we think. They are called…"

"Synchronicity!" Dhimas exclaimed politely.

"Carl Jung invented exactly the right term, didn't he?" Ruben smiled.

"And we have just experienced the most extraordinary act of synchronicity."

"Synchronicity is a profound act of communication at the level of pure consciousness. It is a gift from the Great Architect. If we try to study it as a process of cause and effect then it makes no sense at all. These various coincidences have nothing to do with any causal process."

"I see. We each began with our own separate, independent histories. But now we're part of the same network. The only difference is that Supernova realized this before the rest of us did."

Ruben suddenly exploded with laughter. "All this time I've been trying to understand things in a scientific way. How stupid I was! I'm a fool! An imbecile!"

"Ruben, I hope all this isn't driving you crazy. It is hard enough for me to be gay, I couldn't bear it if anything happened to you."

"Supernova is right. Everything is one vast network and I'm part of it too. I can't stand outside and explain it. Science deals with discrete phenomena, but consciousness is not a phenomenon. All phenomena, including science itself, exist within consciousness itself. We need to find a form of science that is compatible with consciousness. That's the key to everything! In its purest form, science has no preconditions. It is open to everyone, without exception."

Dhimas smiled. "You are sane. In fact, you've never been as sane as you are at this moment."

"Copernicus changed the way we think about the world. He pointed out that the world goes around the sun, not the other way around. But I want to take this one step further. Although this not true geographically, in the most profound sense we are the center of the universe. And we are the center because…"

"We are its meaning."

The two men embraced each other. They stared out the window at the constellations in the sky, and saw themselves reflected in every direction.

33

You are Everything

The curtains of the windows of the house across the road were shut. The day had come and, obviously, Supernova didn't enjoy farewells. She had left a note on his front door.

You are part of everything. Everything is part of you.
Including me.

The pain was intense, even though Ferré knew that they would never be apart. In the background, he could faintly hear the record playing. He wanted Diva, wanted to hold her, wanted to dance with her to the beautiful words:

"Love is free, free is love./ Love is living, living love."

But who could ever stop the Falling Star? She had come for a brief time and lit up his sky. And now he held the key to that light himself. Ferré closed his eyes. A beautiful feeling spread through his soul. Lifted him up. Merged with the morning sky.

Look at me, Princess. I'm flying, high in the sky. Beyond
all reason. We should never be afraid of love. It is
present throughout the whole universe. I am Love.

Dhimas and Ruben

The room was beginning to feel crowded. Piles of books and scraps of paper covered almost every inch of the floor. There was only enough space left for the two men.

"Ten years, Dhimas."

"And we've traveled further than we could ever have imagined."

For a few moments, they enjoyed their sense of euphoria. Then, suddenly, something troubled Dhimas.

"Ruben, Supernova was one of the characters in our story, wasn't she?"

"Of course. Why?"

"Maybe we were characters in our story, too. Why do you think we were there?"

Ruben did not reply. The concept was so amazing he could not even comprehend it.

""What if we weren't writing the story at all? What if we were only dolls in the hands of some greater puppet master? Two men without surnames, living in the molecules of another author's mind, unable to ever escape."

"And we will cease to exist once the last page has been reached."

"And… and… we've never even left this house."

"Two men with no surnames, set to work writing a story in a room, and caught forever in someone else's mind."

"What if the author forgot all about us?"

"We'd be finished."

They looked at each other.

"Ruben…"

"Yes?"

"I love you."

"I beg your pardon?"

"I want to finish in love."

"I love you too."

They held hands tightly. Two men with no surnames in a room. In love with each other.

THE BEGINNING

Further Reading

Bangs, Richard and Christian Kallen. *Rivergods: Exploring the World's Great Rivers*. San Francisco: Sierra Club Books, 1986.

Blackmore, Susan. *The Meme Machine*. New York: Oxford, 1999.

Bohm, David and F. David Peat: *Science, Order and Creativity*. New York: Bantam, 1987.

Brodle, Richard. *Virus of the Mind: The New Science of the Meme*. Seattle: Integral Press, 1996.

Briggs, John and F. David Peat. *Turbulent Mirror: An Illustrated Guide to Chaos Theory and the Science of Wholeness*. New York: Harper and Row, 1989.

Chopra, Deepak. *How to Know God: The Soul's Journey into the Mystery of Mysteries*. New York: Harmony Books, 2000.

De Mello, Anthony. *Awareness: A De Mello Spirituality Conference in His Own Words*. New York: Image Books, 1990.

Ferris, Timothy. *The Whole Shebang: A State of the Universe(s) Report*. New York: Simon and Schuster, 1997.

Gleick, James. *Chaos: Making a New Science*. New York: Viking, 1987.

Goswami, Amit, Maggie Goswami and Richard E. Reed: *The Self-Aware Universe: How Consciousness Creates the Material World*. New York: J.P. Tarcher, 1998.

Greider, William. *One World, Ready or Not: The Manic Logic of Global Capitalism*. New York: Touchstone, 1998.

Helicon Books. *Hutchinson Encyclopedia of Science*. Great Britain: Helicon Publishing, 1998.

Hofstadter, Douglas R. *Metamagical Moments: Questing for the Essence of Mind and Matter*. Toronto: Bantam, 1985.

Krishnamurti, Jiddu. *Freedom from the Known*. San Francisco: Harper, 1975.

Magnis-Suseno, Franz. *Pemikiran Karl Marx* (The Thought of Karl Marx). Jakarta: Gramedia Pustaka Utama, 2000.

Mangunwijaya, Y. B. *Manusia Pascamodern, Semesta, dan Tuhan* (Postmodern Man, Nature and God). Yogyakarta: Kanisius, 1999.

Margulis, Lynn and Dorion Sagan. *Microcosmos.* New York: Summit Books, 1986.

Peat, F. David. *Synchronicity: The Bridge Between Matter and Mind.* New York: Bantam Books, 1987.

Piliang, Yasraf Amir. *Sebuah Dunia yang Dilipat* (A World Folded Back on Itself). Bandung: Mizan, 1998.

Vaughan-Lee, Llewellyn. *Travelling the Path of Love: Sayings of the Sufi Masters.* London: Golden Sufi Centre, 1995.

Walsch, Neale Donald. *Conversations with God: An Uncommon Dialogue* (Book 1). New York: Putnam, 1995.

Wilson, Edward O. *Consilience: The Unity of Knowledge.* New York: Vintage, 1998.

_____. *Conversations with God: An Uncommon Dialogue* (Book 2). London: Hodder & Stoughton, 1997.

_____. *Conversations with God: An Uncommon Dialogue* (Book 3). London: Hodder & Stoughton, 1998.

About the Author

Dewi Lestari was born in Bandung on January 20, 1976 and is a graduate of Parahyangan University (Bandung) in International Relations. Dee, both her pen name and as she is popularly known, first came to public attention through her membership of the pop group "RSD", an abreviation of the names of the three singers:
Rita, Sita, Dewi. She recorded four albums with the group, as well as two solo albums: *Out of Shell* (2006) and *Rectoverso* (2008).

Supernova: The Knight, the Princess and the Falling Star (2001) is the first book in a proposed series of six novels. In its first two weeks of publication, the novel sold 14,000 copies, making it the fastest-selling Indonesian novel to date, and has continued to sell phenomenally well since then. Subsequent volumes in the series include *Supernova: Akar* (Supernova: Roots, 2002) and *Supernova: Petir* (Supernova: Thunderbolt, 2004). These three volumes together have sold more than 200,000 copies.

Dee is also the author of two collections of short stories: *Filosofi Kopi* (*The Philosophy of Coffee*, 2006), recognised as the Best Literary Work of 2006 by *Tempo* newsmagazine and *Rectoverso* (2008). Her recent work is a novel *Perahu Kertas* (*Paper Boats*, 2009). In 2008 she was recognized by *Prestige* magazine as "Writer of the Year" and both in 2009 and 2010 was listed by *Globe Asia* magazine as one of the 100 most influential women in Asia.

Dee has spoken at many international writers' festivals, including the Ubud Writers' Festival, Bali (2004, 2005 and 2010), and the Byron Bay Writers Festival, Australia (2006). She is married and has two children.